Stories I Told Myself

From Humor to Horror

Charles Tabb

Gifted Time Books
Beaverdam, VA 23015

ISBN: 13: 9781797884035

Novels by Charles Tabb

Literary

Floating Twigs
Finding Twigs
Gathering Twigs
Canaries' Song

Detective Tony Pantera Series

Hell is Empty
The Purger
The Whirligig of Time

Coming in 2023:

Saving Twigs

For Bill, George, and Rick, my brothers, with whom I've shared some wonderful times. It's the memories that make us who we are. Because of that, you've helped me become who I am.

ACKNOWLEDGMENTS

Thank you to my Beta readers, Sue, Chuck, and Trisha. Your advice and hard work as you read my manuscripts are invaluable.

Thanks to my wife, Dee, also a Beta reader, who allows me to pursue my dream of writing and offers loving, yet honest, critiques of my work. The muses are difficult task-masters, and they must be satisfied. You allow that to happen.

Thank you to the members of Hanover Writers Club, a chapter of the Virginia Writers Club. You help keep me sane. It's hard to explain the various obstacles we writer's face, but you understand, especially my dear friend, Harry Heckel.

Cover art by Heather Heckel, with photo (ID 250841346) by Nandovidal81 on Dreamstime.com.

Finally, an enormous thanks to you, dear reader. I write for myself, but I keep you in mind with each word. I hope you enjoy the stories, personal essays, and the few poems you will find in this book. If you like what I've written, please feel free to recommend it to friends and write a short review at Goodreads and Amazon. Also, you can order my other novels, which are listed on a preceding page, at charlestabb.com/books. I hope you like them!

I write because, if I don't, the muses will haunt me.

—Charles Tabb

Yet by your gracious patience,
I will a round unvarnished tale deliver.

—Shakespeare, *Othello*, I, iii

And so, from hour to hour, we ripe and ripe,
And then from hour to hour, we rot and rot;
And thereby hangs a tale.

—Shakespeare, *As You Like It*, II, ii

AUTHOR FOREWORD

These stories were written over many years. Some are old, some are new. Some are good, some may be—well—not so good. The appreciation is mostly up to you, the reader. Enjoyment of fiction, like enjoyment of any art form, is a matter of taste. Some stories make us smile while others might disturb us in ways we didn't expect, shading our opinion of the work.

Because of that variation in tastes, I have put these stories in sections, depending on the type of story it is. Each section has a different title. This way, readers who don't care for horror stories can simply avoid that section or read it first if you like that genre.

In any case, I hope you enjoy what I have here. I've said many times that I write because if I don't the muses will haunt me, and my taste in fiction is varied, just as my taste in food is. But always in the back of my mind, I am trying to please my readers in whatever genre I'm writing. These readers have become many, much to my surprise. I would recommend that if you're not a fan of a genre, you should avoid that one.

If you like what you *choose* to read here, please leave a short review on Amazon or Goodreads. If you don't—well I hope that's a matter of taste and not talent.

All this talk of taste reminds me of something that happened when I was a child. A friend and I argued over who was the best band, The Beatles (my choice) or The Dave Clark Five. We were both right in our own way, though I think it could be argued that I was more right than my friend due to the opinion of the extreme majority. See? It's all a matter of taste.

June 2, 2022
Ocracoke, North Carolina

LITERARY/MAINSTREAM

HUMOR

SUSPENSE/CRIME

HORROR

POETRY AND PERSONAL ESSAYS

NOVEL EXCERPT

LITERARY/
MAINSTREAM

WE NEED TO TALK

This story first appeared in the online literary journal Ariel Chart on July 2, 2018.

Author's note: This is the first item I ever wrote that was accepted for publication. I submitted it to Ariel Chart, and the acceptance came the same day, a quick response by any standard. It's funny how ideas just come out of other experiences. This one was converted from a master's level class I took on writing for the theater. It was originally a monologue that I later turned into this flash fiction story, keeping most of the monologue aspects. It remains one of my favorites.

Debbie decided it was time she talked to Bill about what she wanted. Needed, really. She should matter, too.

She watched him peering over his glasses at the TV. They sat in their gray fabric chairs, as they did every night, the seats long ago molded to their bodies. This thought brought images of coffins, and she wondered if they, too, eventually reshaped themselves to fit their eternal occupants.

Bill's graying hair had thinned to wisps. His jowls sagged, and his stomach folded over his belt. She remembered running fingers through thick locks of hair and feeling the muscles in his face when they kissed. She'd changed, too. Her svelte figure had been replaced by wide hips and thighs, and her graying hair hung in dull strands no matter what she tried.

Time was running out. It was now or never.

"Bill, honey, we need to talk. Could you turn off ESPN for a few minutes? The same thing will be on in another hour. Or just record it if it's that important. — No, you can't just mute it because then you'll just watch it without the sound. — Because we need to talk. — No, I don't want any ice cream. I want to talk. — Yes, it's *that* important. I was talking to Hunter the other day and he agreed I should talk with you. — Yes, he called. He's doing fine. — Yes, he said he'd see you at the game this weekend. Honey, we really need to talk."

She steeled herself for what she knew he'd say. "You know how we always used to talk about going on a tour of Europe? — I know it's expensive, but you know it's a dream I've had for, well, forever, it seems. — Where are you going? — No, sit down, please, and listen. I said I don't want any ice cream. — No, you can't have any right now either. We really need to talk about this. — Because it's on my bucket list. There's this festival in Paris this summer where everyone dresses up in period costume. You know, like Marie Antoinette or Louis XIV, and it sounds like fun."

His question caught her by surprise. "My physical? — Yes, I . . . talked to my doctor about the results. — Yesterday. — I'm not talking about that now. I'm talking about going to Europe. — Not now. I'll tell you later. I want to go to Europe."

She paused as her voice caught, and she looked

at the floor, realizing what she'd always known. She pressed on nonetheless.

"I want to do that one thing. Just that one."

Looking back at him, she pleaded with her eyes, but as her father had warned, Bill was Bill. He'd do what he wanted. Her sigh sounded like a dying breath.

"Okay, fine. Never mind. You can turn your ESPN back on."

She hefted herself from the chair, resigned to the habit of her life as the TV blared again. "How about some ice cream?" she asked.

NOT TODAY

This story was initially written years ago but I lost the manuscript. I re-wrote it a couple of years ago. It arose from the idea that the survival instinct is the strongest one we have. A special shout-out to my high school buddy, John Erdmann, who gave me permission to use his name in this story. I'd refrain from going on long walks in the wilderness, John.

John Erdmann lay on the rocky ground, staring into the sun and wondering what had happened. He had been unconscious for a bit, though he had no idea how long. The truth was he was lucky to be alive. Although they were sore, his arms were mobile. That first discovery helped keep him calm while he concentrated on the rest of his body.

His spine was okay. He knew that because he could feel his extremities, and both legs felt as if they'd been hit with a sledgehammer. When he'd checked his mobility, his legs had screamed at him. That worried him, but he continued taking a mental inventory until all major areas were accounted for. He felt he could try to move into a sitting position. Only then would he be able to assess the damage to his legs. He knew they were broken. The question was how badly and whether he could make it out of this god-forsaken wilderness with the injury. He was at least eight miles from the nearest road and twelve from the nearest town.

He'd been hiking in the Arizona wilderness and had found a narrow path that ran up and along the side of a sheer cliff. He'd noticed the ground below the ledge wasn't that far away, perhaps thirty feet, but he was walking along the edge, trying to be careful. He was nearly to where the trail widened a bit when the hawk hit. One second, his footsteps were growing less tentative as he approached the safety of the wider path. The next, he felt as though someone had punched him between his shoulder blades.

He heard the piercing screech as the raptor hit him, knocking him off-balance and sending him over the rim of the cliff. Sometime later he'd awakened to see the clear blue sky above him as if nothing could possibly be wrong. He knew he'd been unconscious, probably not for long though, since the sun had not seemed to move much. Still, being knocked out meant a concussion. His head was pounding, but that was nothing compared to the pain in his legs.

Still staring at the sky, John searched for the damn bird that had put him there, but he could see nothing but cloudless blue and the rising cliff beside him. What had the bird been thinking? Slamming into a person was almost unheard of, though he'd heard of the rare occurrence.

Closing his eyes for a few seconds to gather his thoughts and courage to move, he edged his elbows toward his sides. He pressed them against the ground and pushed until he was able to sit up by putting his weight on his forearms. *Okay*, he thought, *halfway there*. He pushed harder and managed to get his hands beneath his aching shoulders and moved gingerly into a sitting position. Looking at his legs, he thought he might throw up.

Halfway between the knee and ankle, his left leg was turned at an angle it wasn't designed for. The angle wasn't severe, but it was enough to let John know the leg was definitely broken. His right leg was twisted at the knee so that his shin was no longer aligned with the front of his thigh. Instead, it was turned to align with the inside of his thigh, or nearly so. John wasn't sure if a broken bone was beneath the skin, but the leg, like his left, was useless to him.

He wondered if he would die there. He was stranded in the wilderness of Arizona, not exactly desert, but not the tropics either. He had water, but not enough for more than a day, two if he conserved to the point of a barely manageable dehydration.

He looked up at the sun once again and already felt the thirst taking over. Reaching for his canteen, he sloshed the water around to gauge its volume before opening it and taking a quick swallow. He knew a stream was about six miles away in the direction of the road. Of course, if he planned to live to see it, he needed to start moving, yet knowing that any movement would be excruciating.

John took several deep breaths as he readied himself to turn onto his stomach. His arms and hands were good, and his strength and endurance workouts would help him, but his hips and legs were basically dead weight, meaning his upper torso would need to overcompensate to gain the momentum needed to turn himself onto his stomach. He could turn over—if he didn't pass out from the pain.

Taking the rope that was looped onto his belt, he managed to use his knife to cut a small piece from one end. He considered leaving the rest of the rope behind—it wasn't as if he could do much with it other than what he was doing right now, but he decided to keep it just in case. It occurred to him that *just in case* could be to use it to hang himself before he baked to death in the earthly oven he now found himself in.

Returning his rope to his belt and his knife to its sheath, he placed the small length he'd cut into his mouth and clamped down on it. With a grunt, he flung his right arm and shoulder across his body and rolled onto his stomach. He screamed as a level of pain he'd never felt exploded from both legs, attacking his back and groin, where the muscles clenched into a cramp, throbbing in protest. His cheek pressed against the ground as he inhaled great gulps of air and blew them out through his mouth. Sand, dirt, and small pebbles scattered with each breath. He lay on his stomach, waiting for the pain and cramping to subside before attempting to move again. After a few minutes, the agony once more subsided into mere pain and he wondered again how he would survive this while realizing he probably wouldn't.

Still, he had to try. The survival instinct was like that. Move or die. That was his single choice. His past and his future didn't matter, only the now.

His backpack had separated from him as he

fell, and now he saw it a short distance from where he lay. He thought of a small bottle of liquor that had been inside the canvas bag and wondered if it had survived the fall. He wasn't sure how much it would dull the pain, but he knew it would help some. He'd seen enough movies to know people drank liquor to numb the pain of injury. He hoped it hadn't been a lot of the typical Hollywood garbage.

Lifting his chest from the hard ground, he started walking his upper body on his hands while dragging his lower half. Rockets of pain blasted through him with each move, but he kept going, one hand-step at a time, the rope clenched between his teeth. He finally arrived at the backpack and began rummaging through it, praying the whiskey had survived. He'd wrapped the bottle in several towels in case he accidentally dropped the bag. He hoped it had been enough. His hopes grew when he realized he couldn't smell any liquor and the towels weren't wet. Unwrapping the last towel, he let out a small whoop of joy. The unopened bottle of whiskey was intact. It was only 200 ml, or a half-pint of the precious drink, but it would be enough to help dull the pain until the endorphins fully kicked in.

He also knew that drinking alcohol would tend to dehydrate him, but it was either drink the liquor and be able to move fast enough to get somewhere he could be found or die out here in this emptiness.

Drink or die, he thought as he uncapped the bottle and took a swig, feeling the whiskey burn his throat before it landed in his stomach like a small fireball. While he drank, he checked for more useful supplies in the backpack. He found a few sticks of beef jerky, a couple of granola bars, and a few salt tablets. He transferred these to his pockets, along with a compass with a brightly polished silver back for reflecting light to signal others. There was also a two-inch magnifying glass for starting a fire. Perhaps the sun would come in handy after all. Finally, he grabbed a pair of rock climbing gloves. His palms were already sore from being used like bare feet on the rock floor. Finally, he fished the small bottle of acetaminophen from the bag and swallowed two with a sip of the whiskey.

After taking several swallows, John slipped the whiskey bottle carefully into a back pocket to avoid dragging it along the ground. He was already feeling the effects of the liquor and decided to find out if Hollywood had been right.

As John prepared to begin moving again, he noticed a shadow cross over him. Turning his head to look over his right shoulder, he saw a large bird flying overhead. At first, he wondered if this was the same bird that had tried to kill him. Then he saw two more. Maybe the hawk had brought a couple of friends over to the valley to laugh at the result of his handiwork. *Hey, guys. I knocked one off that narrow path. You shoulda seen him tumble ass over tea-kettle to the ground. Man, I bet that hurt.*

"Yeah, pretty damn funny," John said aloud. Then raising his fist in defiance, he gave the birds the bird.

That was when he realized they weren't hawks. They were vultures. And they were waiting for him to die. *Well*, he thought, *at least it wasn't the bird that put me here.*

"Hate to disappoint you guys, but you won't be feasting on my carcass today," he said, more to hear a human voice than anything else. "Tomorrow? Maybe. But not today."

He began to hand-walk again, dragging his dead legs behind like a couple of tree limbs that had attached themselves to his hips. The pain was bad, but not as debilitating, and he was thankful for whiskey and endorphins.

After pulling himself over the rough terrain for nearly an hour, he stopped, already exhausted. Breathing heavily, he pushed himself back to a sitting position, trying to ignore the fire in his legs, which were now nearly twice their size. The legs of his shorts were tight against his skin, and he wondered if further swelling could lead to problems with circulation.

Taking out his knife, he placed it at the bottom hem to cut the legs of the shorts lengthwise to ease the pressure. Then he stopped. Would that be the best thing to do? Or would it be better to keep the impromptu tourniquet in place? He wasn't a doctor. He'd taken a rudimentary first aid class, one that involved things like bad cuts and snakebites. Nobody had ever mentioned what to do if a hawk slammed into you, causing you to fall and break both legs and your pants were starting to cut into you from the swelling. Was compression best, or was easing the tightness better?

He wasn't sure, so he decided to do nothing for now and think about it while he crawled back to civilization with its doctors and nurses. And water.

His thirst was nearly painful in itself. The low

humidity and heat was sapping every drop of moisture from his body, or it felt that way. His mouth felt the way it sometimes did when he awoke from a night of breathing through his mouth—desert dry.

Putting away the knife for now, he took out the canteen, opened it, and took his second swig of water. He figured at this rate, he would run out of water sometime around midnight, if he was lucky. Next, he pulled out the bottle of whiskey. Untwisting the cap, he raised the bottle in a toast. "God bless Jim Beam." He took two swallows and returned the bottle to his back pocket.

Swinging himself over to his stomach again and ignoring the pain that brought tears to his eyes, he continued his laborious journey.

Forty minutes later, he stopped again, crying from the pain, both from the injuries and the swelling that threatened to tear the shorts by itself. He didn't give a damn what a doctor might say, he was going to cut the shorts to ease the tightness. He trembled as he removed the knife and carefully managed to wedge it inside the left leg hole at the bottom hem. He twisted the knife to turn the blade away from his leg, but the point was still cutting into his skin a bit. He quickly tugged at the knife and sliced into the cotton fabric. The exposed skin bulged through the opening as if trying to escape the pain that was coursing through John's body. Moving the knife farther up the leg, he continued tugging and slicing until he had reached the point where his leg joined his hip. Small cuts dotted his thigh where the knifepoint had pierced the flesh.

For ten minutes, John worked at the shorts, cutting lines in the fabric until nothing but dangling flaps remained. He ignored the blood.

When he was done operating on his shorts, his legs still hurt from the injuries, but at least he didn't feel as if his shorts were amputating his legs.

For ten minutes he sat crying. Filled with self-pity, he took turns hating himself, the bird, the vultures that still floated on the warm breezes high above him, and the ground itself for being so damned hard. He wanted to stop, but he knew that would kill him. If nothing else, he didn't want the vultures to win.

Finally, he stopped crying and took a sip of water, followed by a swallow of booze. He swore he would never allow himself to feel such self-pity again. If he died, he died, but it wouldn't be from giving up. His father had always said people usually set their own limits on their accomplishments. He would not do that now because doing so would bring death in its wake.

As the sun sank below the rim of mountains, the temperatures began to moderate. At first, John welcomed this, but he knew that soon the heat would turn to chill. By midnight, the temperatures would be in the mid-fifties. The low had been forecast as fifty-two. Not freezing, but cold enough to be uncomfortable.

John finally stopped and ate some jerky and a salt tablet, washing them down with a few more swallows of water. He guessed he had gone at least two miles that day so far, maybe close to three. Distances were hard to gauge under the circumstances. His first hundred yards had felt like a mile by itself. His arms ached, and despite the gloves, his palms felt as though he'd been smacking them against a rock for several hours, which in a way he guessed he had. His legs still ached, but the pain wasn't as acute as before, either from the whiskey, endorphins, or both. The swelling had decided to stop after it was no longer inflicting immense pain. Now he just looked as if he had a disease that made his legs grow to nearly twice their size and caused them to twist and bend in new directions. He casually wondered if he would end up in a wheelchair for life or have to learn to walk on prosthetics after his legs were amputated.

His mind drifted, imagining a conversation with the doctor. "Sorry, John. We tried to save them, but they were too far gone. Perhaps if you hadn't cut the shorts."

Similar insane conversations became frequent as he dragged himself along, praying for God to get him through this in one breath while cursing Him with the next. John wouldn't blame God if the Almighty had thrown his hands up in disgust and turned away to let him live or die on his own.

He had been struggling to adjust himself so that he could lean back against a rock to wait for either the desire to continue that night or rest until daybreak. He was leaning toward choosing rest when he heard something that made him wish he'd taken a different route altogether.

From somewhere off to his left, he heard a low growl. It held menace and threat, as if warning him that if he didn't leave, an attack was imminent. He wasn't sure whether it was a wolf or a coyote, but either would be bad news. Still, he hoped for coyote since they were at least smaller than wolves, thus less powerful. Either way it was bad, though, because he would be no match for either. Building that fear more, he realized that both often traveled in packs.

I can't leave, John thought, nearly speaking the words aloud. The growling intensified noticeably, as if it had heard John's thoughts, and he wondered if he had spoken the words after all.

He considered the advantages the animal had, a main one being the ability to see in the night. Being nocturnal, they were able to see as clearly in the night as he did during the day.

Trying to gauge the predator's location by the sound, John reached slowly for his knife. The handle felt warm in his hand. It wasn't a big knife— the blade was only four inches long—but it was razor-sharp, and his only hope. His ability to think and plan his movements were his only advantage. The animal could smell him and his fear. The warning growl, though, was evidence of the animal's fear as well. While animal attacks were rare, even in the wilderness, they had been known to happen, and deaths had been reported more than once.

With a yelping bark, the animal charged. In the meager moonlight, John could see it was a coyote, one that had likely come upon him while hunting and simply reacted to his presence.

John reached toward the coyote as it sailed for him and managed to grasp its ears as it lunged. As he took hold of the fur, the knife fell from his grip, clattering against the rock he sat upon. As he grappled with the coyote, he could feel the knife beneath the edge of his right buttock.

Snarling, ragged coughs of fury assaulted the night while John did his best to maintain his position and hold the animal at bay. He would have to get the knife, but to do that, he would have to let go of the animal's head to free one arm, allowing it to turn and bite his other arm before moving in for the kill.

In the dimness, John could see the bared teeth as the coyote did its best to complete its lunge toward John's throat. John wondered vaguely if the coyote was rabid, knowing it probably was since nearly all coyote attacks were attributable to that and a lone coyote was rare. They typically left humans alone, giving them a wide berth. John pushed the thought away as he struggled to live long enough to be treated for rabies. His field of vision was limited to the jaws that were trying their best to kill him.

John decided he would have to do something to get the knife, or he would die. He knew the coyote would lunge for his throat if he let go entirely, so he would have to endure being bitten somewhere along his arm as he let go with one hand to retrieve the knife. Steeling himself for the pain of a bite, he held on with his left hand as he whipped his right hand away from the throat of the wild animal and slapped the hand down onto the knife.

The animal turned its head and latched onto John's left forearm, sinking its sharp teeth into the flesh. John screamed but did not let go of where he gripped the coyote's neck. He could feel the blood beginning to pour from the wound and the unbelievable power of the jaws as they sank into him and held like a bear trap.

John whipped the knife from below him. Raising it, he plunged down into the coyote's torso between the ribs near its spine, pushing the blade in with all the force he could muster.

The coyote yelped in pain and turned its jaws toward the knife-wielding hand and arm. It managed to sink its teeth into John's arm above the knife, but not with the same power it had attacked before. The wound had obviously weakened the animal, but John knew weakening it wasn't enough. He had to kill the coyote if he expected to live.

Switching the knife to his left hand and feeling the teeth rip the flesh of his right arm, John plunged the blade into the side of the animal again. A final yelp was followed by the coyote's attempt to move away from John. It staggered a few steps and collapsed, twitching twice as it lay there before going completely still.

John stared at the coyote, trying to catch his breath and make his heart stop hammering. He vaguely wondered if this entire episode had been for nothing, and he would die soon from a massive heart attack. He sat back and continued staring at the animal that had done nothing wrong, really, as far as the laws that governed its life were concerned. He'd come upon what he considered an enemy and had lost the fight. John was saddened at the animal's death, but still happy it hadn't been him.

John turned his attention to his new wounds. His left arm had deep punctures. He could make out small tears where the teeth had ripped from the flesh to attack his right arm. The teeth had torn the flesh into inch-long gashes. John removed his shirt, and using his knife, he tore strips from it to bind the gashes in an attempt to stanch the flow of blood. The wounds weren't life-threatening but would require stitches to heal properly.

After fifteen minutes of resting, he thought the flow had nearly stopped. His arms throbbed from the assault, and he wondered how they might feel in the morning and whether or not he could continue dragging his body along the ground.

He closed his eyes and did his best not to think about his predicament, but all he could do was remember a story by Jack London he'd read in high school called, "To Build a Fire." It was about a guy in some arctic area who was trying to build a fire, and everything was going wrong. The man was not ready for the challenges he faced and ended up dying in the wilderness. In addition to other lessons, it was a cautionary tale about being ill-prepared, even poorly trained, for the dangers encountered in nature. John recalled how the teacher had talked about how stories of the time saw nature as cruel and apathetic to man's struggles, and how Nature thought of man as nothing more than another animal inhabiting the earth, like an insect or a turtle. As he contemplated the possibility of dying out here alone, John finally understood what the teacher had meant.

He took several swallows of whiskey and leaned back against the rock, where he finally drifted off, despite the pain. Sometime in the night, he awoke shivering, noticing the moon had moved far while he'd slept. His arms ached, especially when he tried to move them. Deciding it would be better to continue than to remain there waiting for daylight, he struggled to turn himself so he could drag his body along the ground once more. The pain of turning over didn't kill him, so he felt a sense of success.

Pulling himself along, he wondered how far he was from the stream. He thought he should be getting close, and he waited to hear the rush of water in the distance. His canteen was nearly empty, perhaps one or two swallows left. Once the sun came up, the temperature would rise quickly, and thirst would become a major problem. He also considered the stream might not be as clean as it looked, but he would take that chance since the alternative was worse. As he pulled himself along toward the water, the sun began its slow rise above the horizon.

Other than his legs, his body had gone past numb by the time he heard the stream washing over the rocks ahead. He could tell it was still a ways from him, but the sound urged him toward it. As the volume grew, he realized something he'd not considered.

Over the years, the stream had carved out a deep gully in the rock and soil. At some places, the ground plunged as much as thirty feet to the water. Then there was the problem of crossing the stream without the use of his legs.

When he'd made his trek from town, he had crossed the stream on foot. The water wasn't that fast or deep, but it was deep enough he might have trouble now. He might even drown in the process. The rocks on the stream bed were perhaps an arm's length below the surface, and the current was fast enough that it could easily wash him downstream if he lost his grip.

A bridge crossed the ravine downstream where the water wound near the town. He needed somehow to get down to the water to refill his canteen, crawl back up the slope to where he began, then crawl along the hard ground beside the stream to the bridge. Once he arrived there, he would be back in civilization. However, someone would likely be driving along the highway and find him if he could make it across the stream somehow. Figuring out the somehow was the problem.

If he couldn't figure a way to do that, he would have to crawl the entire distance to town, adding several miles to his journey. He doubted he would survive if that was necessary.

Ten minutes later, he was staring down at the rushing water that would be easy enough to cross if he had only one good leg. He heaved a sigh and got to work. After all, thinking about the difficulties awaiting him wouldn't solve anything, so he thanked whatever corner of his mind that had insisted he bring the rope. Without it, getting water would have been impossible. He could see that crossing here would be impossible since the water was too deep, so he would have to climb back up and continue his journey to the bridge near town.

Removing the rope from his belt, he found a rock that had been mired in its spot for centuries while offering a lip where he could attach the rope. After doing that, he dropped the loose end over the side of the embankment. Fresh, cool water waited fifteen feet below him.

John gasped in agony as he hoisted his useless legs over the edge of the rocky wall. After a moment to recover from the pain, he gripped the rope and began lowering himself to the stream hand-under-hand while doing his best to ignore the throbbing in his legs and arms. When he made it to the ground below the ledge, he scrambled to the water's edge, plunged his face into the rushing stream, and guzzled the cool drink.

Pushing himself up from the stream, he fought the urge to vomit the water he'd swallowed too quickly. After a moment his stomach quit its rebellion, and he began to breathe again.

He lay on the shore for a few minutes, getting what rest he could before taking out his canteen and filling it. He took more leisurely swallows of the stream's water directly from the source before turning himself around and dragging himself to the end of the rope. Grasping it, he pulled himself up to where he would be standing if not for the uselessness of his legs and looked around before beginning the arduous climb. What he saw made him nearly lose his grip on the rope.

A tree had fallen across the gully about fifty yards upstream from where he was. The tree reached all the way across the narrow gorge. It didn't look wide enough to use it as a makeshift bridge, which would be useless to him anyway, but it did look solid enough to anchor himself with the rope, allowing him to pull his way to the other side. His fear of being washed downriver and possibly drowning was eased. The tree would provide an anchor, provided termites and rot hadn't destroyed its firmness. The wall on the opposite side of the stream was nearly seven feet shorter than the side of his approach. This caused the tree to stretch across the ravine at a fairly sharp angle.

The vision of the fallen tree brought tears to his eyes. For the first time since being hit by the hawk, he felt real joy. His muscles gained a stamina they'd lacked before.

He began to pull himself up the wall, his legs dangling. Using a hand-over-hand motion, he grunted each inch up the slope until he finally grabbed the rock where he'd tied the rope. Then hoisting himself the remaining foot or so, he eased himself down beside the boulder and let out a whoop, ignoring the pain shooting through his legs.

Glancing along the ravine's edge toward the fallen tree, he couldn't see where it crossed the small chasm. Small brush blocked his view. He untied the rope and pulled himself along toward his unexpected lifesaver.

When he arrived, he quickly draped the rope over the fallen tree and moved to the edge of the gulch, allowing his legs to dangle over the edge once again. Just as he turned onto his belly to hold himself on the ledge with his elbows to gather some of the slack that lay between his hands and the tree's trunk, a sound from less than three feet away made him freeze. The quick shh-shh-shh-shh of a rattlesnake broke the silence. John slowly turned his head toward the sound.

A large, coiled diamondback peered back at him. The tongue, which allowed the snake to sniff the air, slithered out, flicked, and slid back. Maybe it could smell his fear. Perhaps it could smell his strong desire to get away. Or maybe it was mistaking those scents for evil intent. Time stopped as they continued to stare at each other. The snake's tongue did its dance over and over, the snake's rattle continued its angry whispers, John remained frozen.

John was sure the snake was going to strike at any moment. It would sink its fangs into his face, injecting the deadly poison. If John had a quick way back into town, the bite would be painful and cause damage without killing him. Antivenom was available there. But in his situation, he would likely die before he could even reach the road.

The snake began to draw back, coiling itself tighter. It was apparently done fooling around with its sudden human visitor and was going to end the standoff. John glanced at the slack in the rope, thankful he hadn't had time to gather it. Just as the snake finished its coil, John held fast to the rope and allowed himself to drop from the ledge into the emptiness below. The snake missed him by less than an inch. John swung like a pendulum from the fallen tree, hanging there while his heartbeat slowed and clear thought returned. The rope's two ends lay coiled like a snake on the rocky shore below.

Using the same hand-under-hand method, he lowered himself to the narrow shore and took a moment to recover from his latest ordeal. Lying on his back, he gathered most of the slack and flicked at the rope, causing it to make small jumps toward the middle of the trunk. It worked better than he'd hoped. He tied the ends of the rope around his waist and eased himself into the cold water.

The water was shallower here, and he began pulling himself along the stream bed toward the opposite shore. Each time he was able to steady himself, he would reach up and flip the rope, the momentum running up the length to cause the rope to hop along the sloped tree trunk. Several times he laughed out loud at the ease of what he thought would be difficult.

Soon, he was at the opposite shore and pulling himself up to where the rope waited, looped around the narrower end of the tree. Crawling up and hoisting himself over the edge to remove the rope from the tree, he secured it to his belt and began crawling in the direction of the road.

As he crawled, he began to think about the story he would be able to tell and wondered if anyone would believe it. First the hawk, then the coyote, and finally the rattlesnake, not to mention the sheer agony and difficulty of the journey itself. He hoped that would be all to the story besides being found alive in time to live.

After an hour or so, he felt a vibration in the ground. At first, he thought it was an earthquake. He prayed if he died in a quake, people would realize that Mother Nature had tried to kill him three times in the past twenty-four hours and had finally sent an earthquake to finish the job. The irony nearly made him laugh.

Then he realized what the trembling was. He grinned then laughed out loud as the sound of the eighteen-wheeler rumbled along.

The road.

And at least one truck had just passed by. *Where there's one, there's more*, John thought.

Twenty minutes later, he arrived at the strip of asphalt heaven. He lay there, unable or unwilling to move. He wasn't sure which. He even welcomed the burning on his hands through the now threadbare gloves as he touched the highway's surface.

He continued to lay there, hoping someone— anyone—would come along soon and find him there, still alive despite all that had happened.

Clyde Benson was taking the curves faster than he should. He knew that but kept his speed anyway. He'd traveled this stretch for over thirty years now and knew every inch of the highway. His Freightliner knew the road, too. He'd be home soon, and Lainey, short for Elaine, would have that night's supper cooking. She was a good cook—he had the stomach to prove it—and the thought of bedtime occurred to him as well, bringing a smile.

When he came around the curve just a few miles from home, he spotted something he'd never seen on before. Some nut was lying half on the pavement. "What the--!" he began, not finishing his exclamation because Lainey didn't like for him to cuss, at least not the word that had nearly escaped.

As he barreled toward what he thought might be a corpse abandoned on the side of the highway, he saw the man move his head and smile up at him. The guy looked half dead, which was somehow worse.

Clyde swerved, managing to hold the truck on the road, and reached for the cord and pulled hard, sounding the Freightliner's horn. As he did this, he stood on the brakes, causing the tires to lock and the smell of burnt rubber to fill the air. Smoke rose from the pavement where his tire's streaks painted the road. There was nowhere to pull over, so he left the eighteen-wheeler idling on the mostly empty highway and jumped out of the cab. Running toward the man, he yelled, "What the hell happened to you?"

He stared at the man lying half on the road. His arms were crudely bandaged, dried blood caking the rags tied there. His lips were swollen and chapped. Finally, Clyde noticed the man's legs and winced. He wasn't sure what had happened, but he knew the man had nearly died from it.

Pulling out his phone, Clyde called 9-1-1. Soon the ambulance arrived and treated John before loading him into the back.

"So, what happened to you, fella?" Clyde asked again as the medics began their work.

John looked at the man who had saved his life. He didn't even know the guy's name. "Long story," John said, happy to have someone besides the vultures and himself to talk to. "If I live, I'll tell you about it one day over a drink." Then he added, "on

25

me."

A week later, John was released from the hospital. The local TV stations had carried his story, and it had been picked up by the networks and a variety of syndicated shows that dealt with odd occurrences. He'd turned down the many offers to do a show about his adventure, as they called it. Somehow, he didn't think it was right to make money off of almost dying. Besides, their constant use of the word *adventure* made him cringe.

Sixteen months after being released from the hospital, John walked all the way out to where he'd been found on the side of the road and started walking into the wilderness once again. By the time he stopped, he was standing where he'd found himself after waking from the fall. The walk had taken him a little over three hours. His legs were sore, but he was alive. He looked up into the blue sky and felt the heat of the sun on his face.

Three vultures were circling overhead.

"Not today either, guys," he said, grinning into the bright sunlight.

THE IN-LAW

Author's note: This story grew from a relationship that I witnessed in which the husband was all talk and no action regarding his future, though the real situation did not turn out the way the story did. The couple did eventually divorce and both people are, as far as I know, happy now. The story became another question of "what if?" in which I asked what would happen if...well, read for yourself. A word of warning to those who are uncomfortable with adult language: This story contains some because, well, that's how some people talk.

Courtney wasn't sure how her mother would handle this. Courtney had been married to Jim for only a couple of years, but it had grown all too obvious the marriage had been a monumental mistake. She was still young, only twenty-five, and the idea of staying with Jim had grown to sound more like a prison sentence than a life together. Only by living with him had she realized that his talk was just that. He had no desire to follow through on his plans. Or maybe he had the desire, just not the motivation to get off his ass and take steps to accomplish anything.

Her mother, of course, loved Jim, but then she had always been a sucker for a good-looking man with sweet-sounding lies. Courtney had spoken to her twin sister Beth just before calling their mom. She'd needed to try out the news on her first to get suggestions on how to break it to their mother. They'd always been like that, each recognizing their mother's penchant for going off the deep end when receiving news she didn't like. In the end, Beth had said, "Just say it quick, like ripping a Band-Aid off." So that's what Courtney did.

"It's over, Mom," Courtney said when her mother answered.

"What's over?"

Okay, maybe that was a little too fast. "The marriage, Mom. It's over. I'm leaving Jim, and I won't change my mind."

Silence. *Calm before the storm?* Courtney wondered.

"Why on earth would you want to do that? He's good to you."

"Mom, he's a shit, mostly, but you don't know about that part."

"Courtney, you know I don't like it when you cuss."

"Get off it, Mom. You use that word a dozen times a day, and in case you haven't noticed, I'm over twenty-one, so I can cuss if I want to. And right now, I fucking want to." Alright, maybe she was laying it on a bit thick, but her mother needed to realize she was an adult and her own person. It would be important she do that if she was going to accept Courtney's decision.

Courtney listened to her mother's sigh, one suggesting she was forced to bear the worst burdens of the world. Her mother went on. "So, then, tell me how it is that Jim is such a bad person. Does he hit you?"

"No, Mother. He doesn't hit me."

"Does he cheat on you?"

"There's more to being a shit than cheating on or hitting a woman, you know."

"Then explain."

"Well, it's not that easy, really. He's—" Courtney thought for a second. "He's all talk and no action."

"Oh," her mother said. "I'm not sure I want to talk about that."

Leave it to Mom to jump to the wrong conclusion. "It's not sex, Mom. If marriage was all about sex, we'd be doing just fine."

"I told you I don't want to talk about that."

"It's that he makes these grand plans for himself. Going back to college. Getting a better job. Being, well, a big shot of some sort. The problem is, he never really does anything. He just, you know, talks about doing something. All talk and no action."

"Sweetheart, these things take time. It's not like he can just go out and find a better job just because he wants to."

"Mom, it's been almost three years. He still works at a 7-11. The only reason he's gotten a raise is they raised the minimum wage. I finished my degree. Why can't he?"

"First, there's nothing wrong with working at 7-11. It's a reputable company. Maybe he's figuring out what he wants to do before investing all that money in a degree."

"I know it's reputable, and if he were trying to move up into management, maybe I wouldn't be so angry, but he's happy just being a clerk in the store. Besides, he knows what he wants to do, or at least he says he does. He says he wants to work in finance. Be a Wall Street investment banker or something."

"Well, there you go. 'Or something.' He's not entirely sure yet."

"Why do you always make excuses for him?"

"I don't make excuses. I just understand getting ahead is more difficult than you think."

"Never mind, Mom. You don't understand. I'm sorry I bothered you. I just wanted you to know, that's all."

She would never convince her mother about Jim. Like herself, her mother had been taken in by all the wonderful plans for his future. But Courtney had lived with him for the past several years, and she'd figured him out. All talk, no action. He was lazy. Content with a dead-end job that required a minimum of actual work.

She had finished her bachelor's and was working on her law degree. She would finish that in May and had already been promised a job with a local law firm. She planned to pass the bar exam on the first try. No easy task, but she could handle it. By then she would be earning a good living. She did not plan to support a convenience store clerk the rest of her life.

"I just think you're being rash," Mom said, "but that's you. Quick-call Courtney."

Courtney stifled a scream. Her mother knew

she hated that nickname, earned when Courtney was thirteen and decided her sister had been in an accident because she was nearly an hour late getting home from her friend Sara's house. She had panicked to the point of calling the police, convincing herself that twins just knew these things instinctively. Beth had walked in the door fifteen minutes after the police were called. Beth's ride had suffered a flat tire, and they had to wait for AAA to send someone.

The tone of Courtney's response dripped with the effort to control herself. "You know I hate being called 'Quick-call Courtney.'"

"Well, you do make sudden decisions, dear. Your father's mother was like that, too, so you come by it naturally, I guess."

Courtney ignored the remark. "I just wanted you to know I would be telling Jim today that I want a divorce. I knew he might call you, so I wanted to call you first."

"Well, Jim's own mother died."

"She didn't die, Mom. She just left and never came back."

"Same thing," her mother said. "So, you've not told Jim yet?"

"No. I'm telling him this evening."

"Then there's still time to change your mind."

"Not gonna happen, Mom."

"Well, think it about it, Courtney. This is a big decision, and Jim's really a wonderful man."

"I've thought about it. He's not so wonderful. He's moving out tonight. I even packed him a bag," she said, holding up a finger to count off each statement despite the fact her mother couldn't see her.

"Well, if he wants to talk to someone, tell him to call me."

"I'm sure I won't have to do that, Mom. He'll call you without any prompting from me. The two of you can feel sorry for him."

After Courtney disconnected the call, she sat staring out her living room window. Tears stung her eyes as she wondered why her mother couldn't be on her side in this. She knew her mother liked Jim, loved him in fact, as she had reminded anyone who would listen countless times. But why would she take his side in this? Didn't she want her daughter to be happy? She had supported her mother's decision to divorce her father, after all. It was time to return the favor.

Headlights swung into the driveway. Courtney glanced at the suitcase beside the door and decided that was too much, sort of like how she first told her mother. Hurrying to the bag, she hefted it into the guest room before Jim waltzed through the front door.

"Lucy, I'm home!" he said, his standard joke, doing his best to imitate the late Desi Arnaz. It was another thing she wouldn't miss.

"Be right out," she called.

When she entered the living room, he had already turned on the TV and was seated in his favorite chair. He had his empty hand raised and curled as if holding an invisible can of beer. He smiled at her, as if fetching his beer was the highlight of her day.

She stared down at him, thinking he would have to leave soon or die. He noticed her gaze and said, "What's the problem?" For Jim there were no problems as long as he was comfortable in his chair.

"You can get your own beer from now on, Jim. I'm tired of being your golden retriever." She was proud of herself for not cussing.

"I thought you liked getting my beer for me."

"The first few times, maybe, but since then it's become just another chore."

"Oh," he said. Grasping her mood, he frowned at her. "Why don't you sit down and tell me about your day?"

She sat in her chair and faced him. "Oh, wait," he said. Rising, he went to the kitchen. When he returned, he had his beer, but he looked put out that he had to get it. He sat down. "Okay, now. What's wrong?" He looked at her as if no problem could be a big one. He was totally clueless about this, and she was suddenly ashamed she'd let it get this far. Her mind was made up, though. He would move out tonight.

She looked at him. "Everything. Everything is wrong."

He actually laughed. "Honey, everything can't be wrong. We're still happy."

Her expression must have clued him in as to how wrong he was.

"Aren't we?" he asked, his face continuing to fall.

"No, Jim. We aren't. One of us is, but the other one is not happy. Not at all."

"You've just had a bad day," he said.

"No, Jim. What I've had is an epiphany. The truth is, it will turn into a bad day if you're still here in an hour."

She looked at him. He said nothing. He just held his beer and stared back at her, the can's sweat starting to drip onto his shirt.

Finally, truth started to dawn. "What are you saying? That you want a divorce?"

She swallowed. This was harder than she'd thought it would be. Her answer came out weaker than she'd intended. "Yes."

"Why?" He was suddenly quite animated. He put the beer down on the table beside his chair and started waving his arms around, something he did when he was agitated. "I still love you! It's not like I cheat on you or stay out late and get drunk. I don't hit you. I'm a good husband!"

Courtney sighed. It would be more difficult convincing Jim than it had been convincing her mother—who still wasn't on board with her decision, Courtney reminded herself. "There's more to being a good husband than not cheating on me or not hitting me," she said for the second time that day.

Jim pointed a finger at her and nearly shouted, "And don't say it's the sex because I know better!"

"It's not the sex either. If all I wanted was sex, you'd be my first choice. It's different. It's—" she stopped and grasped for a word. "It's your laziness. You...you lack something." She frowned herself, unhappy with that description.

"Laziness?! I work a thirty-six-hour week!"

"What do you do with the remaining hours,

Jim?" She did a calculation in her head. "What do you do with the remaining 132 hours in the week?"

He glared at her, offended. "Well, I sleep about eight hours a night, so that's, what? Fifty-six of them."

"Fine," she said, "we're down to seventy-six hours. What about them?"

"I do things," he said, desperation tingeing his voice. "I don't sit around all the time getting fat and watching TV. I—I do things here."

"Like what?"

His head swiveled back and forth, looking for some evidence. "I help keep the house clean!"

"Fine! You spend maybe four hours a week doing stuff around here. It's a small place, so it doesn't take much. That leaves seventy-two hours, Jim. That's three entire days."

"Where are you going with this? What do you expect me to do that I'm not doing?"

"When was the last time you looked for a better job?"

"Is that it? My job? You know I like what I'm doing."

"You're a clerk at 7-11! You make minimum wage!"

"What's wrong with working at 7-11?"

"Nothing if you're a college student or can't find a better job. It's a good job then, but you're capable of more. You keep talking about going back to college and becoming a financial wizard. What happened to that?"

"Is it that I make minimum wage that bothers you?"

"It's more than that, but that is a part of it, yes."

"So? You'll have a job as a lawyer in another couple of months. We'll be fine."

"That's just my point. I don't want to be the chief bread-winner while you work a thirty-six-hour job where you don't have to think. I'll be working, like, sixty or seventy, maybe more." She considered for a moment and added, "Probably more. I'll be exhausted at week's end, and you'll be ready to have fun on your days off."

He looked at her as if she hadn't gotten some point. "But your pay will cover that many hours and compensate you for the exhaustion."

She sat there, stunned, shutting her mouth when she realized it was hanging open.

"Never mind," she finally said. "You're just like my mom. You'll never understand."

"Of course, I'll understand," he said. "Just explain it to me so that I do."

"No, Jim. You won't understand. Your statement about my pay covering my hours shows that."

He sat back and took a long gulp of his beer while keeping an accusing gaze on her. Setting the beer down, he said, "Okay, then. What now?"

"I've got most of your clothes already packed, and I—"

"What?! You already packed my stuff?!"

"Yes. Your suitcase is in the guest room."

Jim turned his can up and chugged the remainder of his beer. Then he marched to the guest room, the only other bedroom in their two-bedroom house, and came out with the stuffed suitcase. "I'll let you know where I am in case you come to your senses!" he said and stomped out the door. Courtney would have found it comical if it weren't so sad.

Sleep was a long time coming that night. She realized she had gotten used to having another body in bed with her. She almost called her sister to come over, but she knew that would only delay the inevitable. She would just have to get used to sleeping alone again. Or get a dog.

The next morning, Courtney got a text from her mom: *Jim is here. He's renting your old room*. She stared at it in disbelief, even checking to make sure it was really from her mother. Jim was staying there? In *her* old bedroom? That was insane. She started to text back and thought better of it. This called for more. She phoned her mom.

"Hello, dear," her mother said as she connected.

"Are you insane?! You're renting my soon-to-be ex-husband *my* old bedroom?! Do you know how damn crazy that sounds when I say it? When I actually speak those words?"

"Don't cuss at me, dear! He had to stay somewhere! He couldn't very well sleep on the street! And he can't exactly afford a hotel."

"He could if he had a better job!"

Courtney could hear Jim in the background. "Is that Courtney? If she wants to speak to me, she should call me, not you."

Courtney screamed into the phone. "Tell him of course, it's me! Who does he think would call you about the fact he's now living in his ex-wife's old bedroom?! Is he as stupid as you are crazy?!"

"You're not his ex-wife yet, dear. These things take time. You know, like finding a better job."

"If it takes as long to divorce him as it has taken him to even think about actually getting off his ass and finding a better job, I'll just save the courts a lot of time and me a lot of money and shoot him!"

"Courtney, I'm going to hang up now. There's no call for any of that. You're being so unreasonable."

"Unreasonable?! Do you have any clue what this feels like? It's as if you've replaced me with him!"

"Nobody has replaced anybody. Calm down! He's just going to stay here until he can afford his own place."

"Is that what he said? Then I'd guess he'll be there when he turns forty at least. Enjoy him, Mom! Oh, and he likes for you to fetch his beer for him like a trained dog!" Courtney wished she had called on a land-line so she could slam the receiver down, but all she could do was press the disconnect button with more force than usual.

She sat there, stewing about the call, running it over in her mind. Then she pressed some buttons to call Beth.

"Hey! I was just think—" Beth began.

"You'll never believe this!" Courtney interrupted. "Never! This is crazy, even for Mom!"

"What happened?"

"Mom is renting my old room to Jim. He's living in my old bedroom!"

"You're joking," Beth answered, though she knew her sister was serious.

"I wish!"

"That's—well—that's insane. Doesn't she realize how crazy that is?"

"Apparently not. She said he couldn't afford a place of his own, and I told her he could if he'd get off his ass and find a better job. She sounded happy about it!"

There was silence on Beth's end for a moment. Then, "I am so sorry, Court. You need me to come over? I can. It's my day off. We can cry on each other's shoulder and eat ice cream like when we were teenagers and a boy broke up with us."

Courtney thought about her offer and decided to say no for now. She would think about all this and try to get a grip on what had become a rather bizarre reality. "Thanks, but not right now. I have to think."

"Well, if you change your mind, let me know. I can be there in a jiffy."

"Thanks, Beth. I'll call you later."

The divorce went through in six months. The service papers had her mother's address on them. So did the final decree. A year after the divorce was final, Jim became Courtney and Beth's stepfather.

As Courtney related this tale to her analyst, whom she had started seeing two months after Jim moved out, she laughed at her analyst's reaction. Courtney knew that a therapist was supposed to be neutral. She knew that they needed to maintain that neutrality regardless of anything the patient might say. Still, her therapist's words were the most comforting ones she'd heard since the day she'd called her mother about the plan to divorce Jim, and while she and Dr. Davidson weren't friends socially, they had come to know each other well.

When Courtney told the therapist that her ex was now her stepfather, Dr. Davidson dropped her pencil and, totally losing her professional demeanor, said, "Are you kidding me?"

THE FIFTH WHEEL

Author's note: This story was written long ago. The seed for this story was wondering what it would be like for someone who felt out of place to actually be the sanest one in the group. After all, we've all felt like a fifth wheel in our lives at some point. What if we're the more normal person there, and the others are all the fifth wheels? Again, this story has some adult content.

Harold stood at the front door to his house wondering what would happen when he went in. He knew he shouldn't be nervous. This was, after all, his wife's family—Barbara's brother and two sisters, with their respective adult children, along with their families. They should all be considered family, but while he tried to think of them that way, he couldn't say the same for their views of him. Frankly, he wasn't sure how they viewed him. Mostly, they ignored him. He'd married Barbara nine years ago, a second marriage for each, but he still felt like an outsider whenever they got together with any of Barbara's family.

Taking a deep breath, Harold opened the door and entered his house. The party was already in full swing. It had become an annual ritual long before he arrived on the scene. The family got together for a big party every spring. They would converge at a

41

family member's house—the hosts changed every year—and get drunk while managing somehow to get back to their own homes or their hotels without having an accident or getting arrested for drunk driving. Harold found it astounding that year after year, they survived without a single mishap.

Harold took in what was usually familiar surroundings. He and his wife were this year's hosts of the Belmont Family Extravaganza. They even referred to it as the BFE. Barbara would talk about "the BFE" in shops and the grocery store, as if everyone knew the meaning. His own home now looked like a foreign country he'd never visited. The layout was the same, but the decorations and atmosphere had turned it into something else entirely.

Colorful streamers floated in arcs below the ceiling, and glitter and confetti were everywhere. He wondered how many times they would need to vacuum and sweep the floors to get it all up. He could picture months of finding bits of the colorful debris like Easter eggs that had never been found. Small bowls of nuts, chips, and candies rested on tables throughout the downstairs, mostly untouched by everyone but the many grandchildren. Barbara had decided to base this year's BFE on a theme, "Nights in Rio!" Posters she'd borrowed from her job as a travel agent—stolen, really—decorated the walls in every room.

Harold was no fool, although many of his in-laws might be. There was a contest at the travel agency to see how many trips to Rio de Janeiro could be booked this summer. The agent who sold the most would get a nice bonus, and Barbara was hoping the posters might plant a few seeds. Harold didn't mind that she was doing this, so long as the missing posters were never discovered. He wondered vaguely if they would end up using the possible bonus to hire someone to de-glitter and de-confetti their home.

He had told Barbara last week he had something important to do the day of the party—at least he could call it important—just to avoid some of it, and he'd managed to delay the inevitable for more than two hours. Walking into the kitchen without being noticed by even one of the thirty-six other people in his house, he saw that every bottle of any kind of alcoholic beverage they had was sitting open on the counter, as if a convention had stopped by to sample what he had in the cabinets. In a way, one had, he thought. A convention of Belmonts. Half-empty bottles of soda stood guard around the liquor.

He left the kitchen and walked through the living room, excusing himself to his wife's relatives as he squeezed between them to make it to the bathroom down the hallway. He spoke to several to be polite, but they barely acknowledged him beyond stepping closer to someone they were talking to so he could pass behind them. A few smiled as if to apologize for the inconvenience the BFE brought, but mostly they acted as if they had hired him to cater the event. Of course, had there been a caterer, he would have been doing the hiring. Rule one was that the host family paid for the shindig.

This reminded him of the BFE two years ago

hosted by Mallory, Barbara's older sister. He and Barbara had traveled over three hundred miles to be treated to chips and dips and Old Milwaukee beer. That was the sum of everything provided. Mallory's husband, Doug, was an attorney and could afford more than Harold, who was an accountant, but that year's BFE had been more like a college frat party done on the cheap. There had been only two large bags each of three different kinds of chips and five small containers of various kinds of dip. They'd run out of everything but the beer, which Doug kept stored in his garage in stacks ten cases high, but that was the norm at Doug and Mallory's. The truth was Harold could almost feel Doug cringe every time someone opened another can of Old Mil', as if each sound of a beer pop-top was the chime on an old-fashioned cash register.

Harold had complained to Barbara about Doug and her sister being such cheapskates, but she'd dismissed it, saying that Doug was sometimes frugal to a fault. To a fault? More like to a failing.

The odd thing was that the lack of food or any beverages besides Old Milwaukee and iced tea had not been the subject of a single conversation, either at the party that night or in the weeks and months following. It had not been so much as mentioned by anyone. When he had broached the subject with Frank, his wife's brother, a month after the event, Frank had looked at him as if Harold had somehow misremembered the party. The look on Frank's face had suggested he and his family had eaten at Doug's BFE better than they had in weeks.

Barbara's plan for tonight involved heavy hors

d'oeuvres, complete with two spiral-sliced hams, broiled potatoes, steamed asparagus, and various kinds of breads and desserts. The asparagus alone cost more than the entire contingent of chips and dips at Doug and Mallory's hosted event. And the twelve-year-old Scotch Mallory had insisted upon, plus the various other expensive liquors, made Harold want to file for bankruptcy.

Harold found a line of four people at the bathroom and decided to use their private bath in the master suite upstairs. Squeezing again between people and the wall, he managed to get upstairs and relaxed once he arrived at his and Barbara's bathroom. When the doorknob refused to turn, he wanted to scream.

Knocking lightly, he said, "Barbara? You in there?"

He heard rustling and subdued conversation. Then, "Be out in a minute." It was Gail, Barbara's younger sister. After about a minute, she came out of the bathroom. Alone.

"Who was with you?" Harold asked, confused.

She stared at him as if he'd implied that she had a truck in there. "What?"

"I heard you talking with someone when I knocked. Someone was in there with you."

"I was on my phone."

Among her other shortcomings, Gail was a terrible liar. He knew someone else was in the bathroom, and what was more, she could see that he knew. "I heard the other person. They definitely weren't on your phone. You were with someone in there."

Gail looked around as if he might be imagining things. "Nobody here but us sisters-in-law."

Harold stepped into the bathroom, looked around, and pulled the shower curtain aside. An embarrassed Doug was in there, hiding. Jerking his thumb over his shoulder, Harold said, "Get out, Doug." Then he turned to them and said, "Find somewhere else to have your affair, okay?"

He didn't care if they screwed around. Hell, if he had been married to any of them besides Barbara, he'd be on the lookout for extra fun himself. He just didn't like it that they were using his bathroom for their love nest.

As he closed the bathroom door on their embarrassment, it occurred to him they were the first people to speak directly to him since he'd entered the house. He'd not even seen Barbara, and he wondered if she had sneaked away with Gail's husband, Jake. *Perhaps I should check the kids' rooms*, he thought, but abandoned the idea when it occurred to him that he might actually find Barbara and Jake and wouldn't have a clue how to handle the awkward situation.

Ignorance is bliss, he reminded himself as he finished his business and walked out.

Heading downstairs again, he saw that Doug and Gail were now separated, as if nothing had happened. Doug was talking to Gail and Jake's son, Tim, and Gail was talking to her brother, Frank. Still no Barbara or Jake. He also hadn't seen Mallory and wondered if she had any clue about her husband's affair with her little sister.

Harold got himself a drink and noticed Doug

46

signaling he wanted to talk to him in private. After catching Harold's eye, Doug jerked his head slightly to one side in a "follow me" gesture and went out the back door into the yard where some of the younger children were enjoying the swimming pool. As they found chairs and sat, Doug's grandson Pete called out, "Grandpa! We should make this the permanent place for the BFE!" Besides hoping this idea was ignored by everyone who might hear it, Harold was amazed that Pete used the initials, reminding him of the way Barbara acted as if the party had been a national event for years.

After taking their seats as far from the rambunctious children as they could, Doug held up his drink, waiting for Harold to clink glasses with him, as if they were not only related by marriage but were also the best of friends. Harold could count the number of times they'd spoken beyond idle pleasantries.

Harold clinked his glass with Doug's to be polite. Doug took a sip from his drink while Harold just sat there, waiting for Doug to start talking. He knew what Doug wanted to talk about, of course, and he wasn't disappointed.

"So, Harry—"

"Harold."

"Whatever. Anyway, I wanted to know what you are considering doing about what you saw."

"Doing?"

"Yeah. I mean, if you go talking about that, you'll just end up hurting a lot of people, from our spouses all the way down to grandkids, like Pete there."

Harold couldn't believe what the man had said. He cleared his throat and said, "Well, I'm not sure what I'll say, if anything, but I gotta ask you something."

"What?"

"Shouldn't you have thought about that before you two became involved?"

Doug's eyebrows shot up in shock while Harold tried to hide his surprise that his brother-in-law was offended by his question.

"Hey, it's not as if we planned this. In fact, today was the first time we did anything at all. I mean, the spark's always been there, you know, but we live about two-hundred miles from each other, so an affair would be difficult, to say the least. I mean, all we did was kiss and, well, grope a little."

"I really don't want to know what you did," Harold said. Looking at Doug, he knew the only way to end this conversation—which neither of them really wanted to have—was for him to agree to say nothing.

"Look, Doug," he said, "I really don't care if the two of you get a hotel room and screw each other's brains out. It might even be a good thing for everyone. I just don't want you sneaking off and finding somewhere in my house to have your fun."

"Really? You won't say anything?"

"No, Doug, I won't."

"What makes you say it might be a good thing if we screwed our brains out?" Doug asked, his smile indicating he thought it would be a good idea, too.

Harold stood up before answering. "Because

then you'd lose what little brains you have and we'd all be done with you both."

He almost laughed at Doug's slack-jawed, silent response. Then Doug's face turned red, but he wasn't drunk enough to ignore what might happen if he responded. After all, Harold had the news of the day, and he'd agreed not to spill it. It wouldn't do for Doug to make him any angrier. Harold could change his mind.

So instead of the outburst he wanted to make, Doug raised his glass in another toast. "Then here's to silence," he said and drained his drink of twelve-year-old Scotch.

When Harold entered the house again, he saw Jake and was surprised how relieved he was not to see Barbara with him. Then he remembered that Gail and Doug had separated upon rejoining the party, so that Jake was there meant nothing. With that thought, he wondered where Barbara could be. He noticed Mallory chatting with Gail and walked up to them.

Gail looked as though she might faint. She obviously thought he was going to tell what had happened.

"Gail? Mallory?" he began. "Enjoying the party?" He gave Gail a glance that said he already knew her answer while conveying that he wouldn't say anything.

"Sure," Mallory said. "The food's really great, and I love how Barbara decorated the place. Rio! Who'd have thought to have a theme? We've never had a theme before. I kinda like it."

Harold could tell Mallory was on her fourth or

fifth drink of scotch and soda, or perhaps she'd already graduated to scotch on the rocks. He could detect only a slight slurring in her speech, but he knew it was only a matter of time before half of what she said would be gibberish. Gail just continued to look nervous, grinning too much and biting one corner of her lower lip.

Suddenly, a voice from behind him startled him. "Yeah, who'd have thought of having a theme for the party?" It was Jake.

"A travel agent," Harold answered, earning him the same looks he usually got when he said something where he was connecting dots the others didn't even see. He'd grown as used to the looks as his wife's family had to his off-the-wall statements. There had been times in the past nine years when he had said something to the group and the room had gone silent, their stares seeming to pin him to the wall as if he'd just passed gas rather loudly. Someone would invariably say something like, "Oh, well, yeah" before the conversation swelled again to normal volume with everyone mostly ignoring Harold.

Finally, Jake actually got the connection. "Oh! Yeah! Of course!" he said, slapping him on the back as if they were old friends. Then, he said, "Hey, maybe she could get some of us a discount or something on a real trip to Rio." Looking at Harold, he added, "You think she could? I mean, we're family, after all."

"I'm sure of it," Harold said. "Where is Barbara, anyway? I've not seen her."

"Oh, she went to the store for pretzels," Jake

said. "Sheila, who was late as usual, looked around as soon as she got here and said, 'Where the hell's the pretzels?' So, Barbara apologized and went to get some." He looked at Harold and said, "I think she tried to call you or something at the office to see if you'd stop for some. You said you'd be there, or at least that's what she said." Jake laughed. "She was none too happy you didn't answer, big fella. She tried your cell, but no luck."

"I was in a meeting with my boss," Harold said, the lie ready. Wasn't in my office, exactly, so the direct line wouldn't reach me."

"Hey, it's not me you gotta convince," Jake said. "I think Barbs thought you were stepping out on her or something." He looked at his wife and said, "Good thing we don't have that to worry about, eh, honey?"

Gail smiled at her husband while casting a glance at Harold. "Of course not, baby!"

Harold thought he might throw up.

At that moment, Barbara stepped through the door carrying two grocery bags of pretzels and more chips. Seeing Harold, she said, "There you are! I tried to call you!"

"He was in a meeting with his boss," Jake said, taking on the unsolicited position of advocating for Harold. "Calls wouldn't have gone to him."

"Craig was working too?" Barbara asked.

"Yes, dear," Harold said. "He's the reason I had to go in." He prayed they wouldn't see Craig anywhere in the next several days. His boss wouldn't like to be part of his lie to Barbara. He didn't like lies, regardless of the reasons behind them. The truth was he'd gone to see a movie rather than put up with the first two hours of the famous BFE.

Handing Harold the grocery bags, she said, "Well, here. Make yourself useful. Open the pretzels and pour them into some bowls, and for God's sake, let Sheila know the damn pretzels have arrived. Who knew she was on some low-fat kick and wouldn't eat any other kinds of snack?"

Harold did as he was told. As he walked to the kitchen for the bowls, he daydreamed about cramming an entire bag of the salty sticks down Sheila's throat while screaming, "Are these enough?! Are these enough?!"

Instead, he strode into the den where he'd seen Sheila earlier and handed her a bowl of pretzels. "Here you are," he said. "Will these be enough?" The words were frighteningly close to his imagined attack on her, and he had to stifle a laugh.

Sheila beamed. "Why yes. You folks didn't have to go to any trouble on my account," she said as if she meant it.

Instead of taking the offered bowl, she grabbed a half-dozen pretzels from it, as if Harold were some sort of waiter. "This will be plenty for now," she said. "I do have to watch my salt, you know."

This nearly sent Harold over the edge. Sheila's insistence on pretzels in the first place had set in motion a series of events that Harold would worry about for days. He and Barbara ran into Craig and his wife at the club several times a week on average. The idea that Sheila's mini-tantrum for pretzels might cause him an unbelievable amount of grief with both Barbara and his boss brought back the fantasy of shoving handfuls of the snack down Sheila's throat. Only this time he had to consciously restrain himself.

"Enjoy them," he said.

He could feel his face muscles doing their best to smile. He wasn't sure what the effort produced, probably something resembling an insane grimace, and it caused Sheila to comment to Doug and Mallory's daughter, Donna, "Is something wrong with Harold?"

Harold heard Donna's snarky reply, "When is there something not wrong with him?"

Harold left the den and aimed for the stairs. He would have to disappear for a while. He feared he might actually attack one of Barbara's siblings or one of their spouses.

When he stepped into their bedroom, he found what he'd mildly suspected all along. Barbara was there, naked from the waist up. Jake was standing before her, his pants around his ankles and his underwear around his knees. Barbara was stroking him while sitting on the bed. She gasped upon seeing Harold, who froze in the open doorway. The three of them knew there was no explanation for this. It could only be what it appeared to be.

Harold said nothing. He simply strode over to the closet and retrieved his suitcase. Walking to the dresser, he began emptying the drawers as if he'd done it every day of his life.

"Oh, Jake, you might want to talk to your wife. I caught her earlier today in our bathroom with Doug," Harold said. "They were definitely not conducting a science experiment either."

"My wife's having an affair with Doug?" Jake asked as if he had the right to be indignant.

"Yep, though I don't think it's gone quite as far as your affair with my wife," Harold said, continuing to pack his bag. Leaving them scrambling to get dressed, he went into the bathroom and gathered his toiletries. Then, he came back into the bedroom, dropped his shaving kit into the suitcase, and snapped the bag shut.

"I'll be back for the rest of my things," Harold said as he left the room. Then turning back to them, he said, "Carry on."

He walked down the stairs and went to find Gail. Finding her in the den with Doug and Mallory, he announced loudly to everyone in the room, "May I have your attention, please? May I have your attention?" Everyone stopped talking, probably because they noticed his suitcase and wondered what was happening. Others from different rooms stuck their heads into the den.

"Thank you. If all the children inside could please go out to the pool." Nobody moved at first, so he added, "Parents, you won't want your children to hear this." He waited as several of the kids scampered outside at the urging of their parents and continued. "I just wanted to announce a few things. First, I just caught my wife giving Jake oral sex, so I'm leaving now." He turned to Mallory. "And Mallory, I caught your husband with your younger sister earlier. They were together in my bathroom upstairs and, as Doug so eloquently put it, 'kissing and groping.'"

Doug stood and pointed an accusing finger at Harold before ending all possibility of denying what had happened. "You said you'd keep quiet!"

"Yes, I did," Harold said. "I guess I lied. So, sue me."

Harold turned and strode out the door amid the complete silence that ensued. As he closed the door behind him, he wondered if liberation had ever felt so good. He could hear the screaming and accusations explode inside his house as he went to his car. He would drive to the local Hilton, where he would stay for the next couple of nights while he got his new life together.

On the drive there, he smiled in a way he hadn't in some time.

Nope, he thought, *liberation never felt this good before*. At least not to him.

SECRETS OF REGRET

Author's note: This story came about when I was thinking about the act of keeping secrets, the effects of confession, and the healing power of forgiveness. We all have secrets, most of them harmless, but we also know that if those affected by a secret knew the truth, damage to a relationship could occur, often damage great enough to end that relationship. I didn't want to write about a couple on the brink of divorce. The kind of secret that kills marriages is all too common and was already addressed in "The Fifth Wheel." I wanted to create two young women whose lives had been close for years and who felt their souls were somehow intertwined and yet, when faced with the idea of telling their biggest secret, at least one found it very difficult to do. It's not a story for children for a number of reasons, but it does raise questions about what we would be willing to tell even our best friend.

Amanda Blair was thankful the interview was nearly over. She had one last question, one of her stock *end of the interview* questions she couldn't wait to get through to get away from Brad Crayfield, the aging rock star with his aging rock band, The Crayfield Brothers. He'd begun the interview asking if she was any good in bed. Her answer, "Good enough not to have to prove it to you or anyone else," had brought laughter and a smirk that lasted the entire hour. She couldn't shake the idea he was assessing her prowess in that area of life with every second, making her want to hit him.

The final question came out with a sigh of relief because in about two minutes she would be leaving. "What is something you believe that others often disagree with?"

He stared into her eyes for a moment and said, "That everyone has secrets they wouldn't tell their best friend. Many of those secrets would make half the people we know abandon us, and some would send even our families running away."

The response caught her by surprise. She had figured he would say something about drugs and how enlightened he felt when he was so stoned that he couldn't see. She gathered her thoughts and decided she couldn't let his answer go by without a comment. "Maybe some people, but not everyone." Her look conveyed the absolute certainty that she had no such secret. She always considered herself an open book, especially to her best friend, Taylor.

"So, then. You're telling me you have no secrets?"

"I didn't say that. I just don't have any I wouldn't share with my best friend."

"Then what you're saying is that your best friend knows everything about you. Is that it?"

"No, but only because I've not shared them with her."

"Why not?"

"Maybe because she hasn't asked." Who was he to start interviewing her, anyway? She was the journalist here. He was just Brad Crayfield of the Crayfield Brothers Band. He'd been much more popular when he was younger than he was now, and most of his success was in the past.

Brad grinned at her, but she could still see the lurid smirk that had been there the entire hour. "Sorry if I hit a nerve, but you've proved my point. So, what you're saying is you have no secret you wouldn't be willing to publish in your magazine?"

"I wouldn't go that far. My magazine isn't my best friend, and neither are our readers."

He gazed at her for a moment, his eyes twinkling with mischief. Finally, he leaned forward and said, "Are you a gambling sort?"

"You mean wager for money?"

"Well, maybe not money. Just, you know, the right to say you're right."

"In other words, a gentleman's bet."

"Or gentlewoman's," he replied, the smirk growing into a cheeky grin.

For some reason, she couldn't let this alone. She wanted to punch him, but the best she could do was to make this bet and prove him wrong. She figured it would have something to do with telling a secret to her best friend, and she had no qualms about that.

"What's the bet?"

"Tell me your deepest secret."

"No way. You're not my best friend, either."

He kept the same smile on his face, one of supreme confidence he would win the bet anyway. "Okay, do you believe your best friend would say the same thing? That she has no secrets she wouldn't tell you?"

Amanda considered this for a moment. She knew Taylor well. They'd been besties, as Taylor called it, since they were in middle school together. Some of the secrets they knew about each other were totally private, the ones nobody else knew or ever would know. She felt she knew or could know any of Taylor's secrets just by asking.

She looked at Brad and said, "Yes."

"Okay, give her a call and ask her to tell you her deepest, darkest secret, one she's never told you before. If she tells you, you win. If she refuses, I do."

She grinned at him. She had this in the bag. She began to wish she'd bet money. Brad Crayfield wasn't exactly poor, has-been or not.

Taking out her phone, she pulled up her recent calls. She'd spoken to Taylor just last night, giving details of a date she'd been looking forward to but which turned out to be a dud. That was ample evidence she would win this stupid bet. Pressing the button to call Taylor back, she gave Brad Crayfield an evil grin.

"Maybe I do want to bet money," she said.

"Well, that's your—" Amanda held up a finger, signaling him to wait.

"Hey!" she said into her phone with more happiness than she felt. "Listen, I'm here with Brad Crayfield and...yes, that Brad Crayfield.... Taylor, stop a second. I have a question." She looked over at Brad and then at the wall to her left. For some reason, she couldn't look at him as she asked Taylor to spill the beans about her darkest secret.

"You see, we have this bet going…. No, not for money, just a bet. Anyway, he believes that everyone has a secret they wouldn't tell their best friend, so I said you'd tell me your deepest, darkest secret, just as I'd tell you mine. So, we made the bet and I'm calling you to get you to tell me your most private secret."

At the other end of the call, Taylor blinked her eyes and sat back in her chair, her work forgotten. Tell Amanda her most private secret? She couldn't. Wouldn't! It was something she barely admitted to herself.

"So, there's no money involved?" Taylor asked.

"No," Amanda answered. There was silence on the phone for a moment. Then Amanda said, "Taylor? You're going to tell me, right? I mean, I'd tell you." Her voice sounded hurt, as if this were a serious breach in their friendship.

"Honey, I can't. I just can't. It's too personal."

Amanda glanced at Brad, whose arrogant grin never faltered. He was taking delight in putting a dent in a friendship she'd had since sixth grade. She wondered if the dent would be irreparable. One thing was certain. She no longer felt as close to Taylor. It was like realizing someone you loved had cheated on you. Without warning, tears of surprise and shock stung.

She swiped at her eyes and said to Taylor, "I guess if you feel that way, he wins." *And I lose*, she thought, *and more than this stupid bet*.

They said awkward good-byes as Amanda ended the call. When she looked at Brad, he had this oh-I'm-so-sorry look on his face, as if he gave a damn.

"Wow, I didn't think it would make you cry. I just thought you'd be pissed I won the bet."

"You really didn't win, you know," she said, working to regain her composure. "I'd tell her anything."

He shrugged, as if the entire episode meant nothing. "You're probably right. We'll call a tie, okay?"

She was suddenly angrier than she'd been in months, maybe years. "Fuck you!" She said, noticing he didn't even have the decency to look surprised at her outburst. Quickly gathering her things, she strode from the hotel lounge where they'd met for the interview. She wanted to throw a chair through the mirror behind the polished bar. Hell, she wanted to throw him through the mirror!

She stormed from the room, the eyes of the few scattered patrons following her. She could see the *what-the-hell-happened?* looks on their faces. She didn't care. Tears were running down her cheeks now, and she hurried to her car. She felt betrayed, as if she'd told Taylor her biggest secret, only to have her blab it to the world.

She sat in her car for ten minutes and cried. When she managed to get some control of herself, she decided she had to talk to Taylor, whether or not she—or Taylor—wanted to.

Amanda pressed the button on her phone and called Taylor back. On the fifth ring, she answered.

"I'm sorry, Hon. Really, I am, but—"

"Lunch?" Amanda asked. She knew even in

that single word Taylor could hear the tears.

"Sure, Babe. Where?"

"Sinthia's?" It was a place with good salads where they often met for lunch or just to talk over tea or a latte. The name was a pun on the owner's name that she used in her ads, "Foods that are sinfully delicious without adding extra padding."

"Okay, Hon. Meet you there around 12:15."

Amanda clicked off and thought about all their times together. They'd always told each other everything, or she'd thought they had. They'd even shared the stories of losing their virginity. Hell, Taylor had even confessed to masturbating when they were fifteen, and while the majority of people did that, they didn't exactly tell everyone about it! But they'd watched a *Sex and the City* episode together on HBO that included it, prompting the confession. What secret could Taylor have that she thought she couldn't share?

She wondered if she was overreacting but decided she wasn't. They had always been so close Amanda had considered them to closest friends in the world. It was a matter of trust, and Taylor's refusal was basically saying she didn't trust Amanda to keep the secret.

As Taylor sat in her office thinking about what had happened, she wondered if she could get the rest of the day off. She no longer felt like doing any work. She'd almost not answered Amanda's last call. She was afraid Amanda would insist she be told her secret, and she just couldn't do that. She'd committed a crime. There was no way she could tell anyone. She knew Amanda must be wondering what had happened that she couldn't confess.

They'd told each other some very personal things in their lives, which was probably what had led Amanda to make the stupid bet in the first place. They'd told everything, that is, except confess to a crime.

She knew Amanda would ask why she hadn't shared her darkest secret. She wanted to tell her they weren't in middle school anymore. That as adults, confessions could have wide-ranging consequences. As kids, their secrets were nothing more than confessions to things that would get them in trouble with their parents, even if they were juvenile crimes. Hell, they'd even shoplifted in a store once on a mutual dare.

Of course, she'd never told Amanda she'd continued shoplifting after that. She wondered if she could confess that and Amanda would drop her little investigation.

Then again, would Amanda buy it that something from so long ago could have started the problem? She doubted it. Still, she could try.

Taylor left for lunch at noon. She'd considered calling and canceling, but she knew it would only be delaying the inevitable. When she entered Sinthia's, she saw Amanda at a table sipping a glass of tea. She approached and sat down, foregoing their usual hug.

As apprehension settled on both young women, Taylor tried a "forgive me" smile. She could tell from Amanda's expression that it didn't work.

"Okay," Taylor began. "Remember that time

we shoplifted on a dare?"

"Yeah."

"Well, I never told you, but I kept doing it."

"That can't be *it*," Amanda said. "For one thing, that's just too small a thing. I mean, who cares about what you did years ago? For another thing, I already knew that."

"You did?"

"Of course. Your family isn't rolling in it, and there's no way you were able to save the money to buy the clothes you were suddenly wearing after that. I mean both our folks shopped at Walmart for clothes. Not a bad place, really, but not the height of fashion, either. Then suddenly you're sporting the latest Abercrombie tops? I was kinda shocked your parents didn't figure it out."

Taylor was suddenly embarrassed. She looked into the hurt eyes and said, "Amanda, I just can't. I could go to—" she stopped. She had nearly revealed that the secret involved a crime. She glanced at Amanda. She had already figured out the word she'd not said.

"Oh, my God! You committed a crime?"

Taylor looked around the room, first wondering if anyone heard Amanda's question, then trying to decide if she could just get up and run out. That would never work, though. Amanda was not one to let go of something so easily. She would come to Taylor's workplace to find out what had happened. The same thing that made Amanda a journalist wouldn't allow her to let it go.

Blushing and trying to swallow the lump of shame in her throat, Taylor nodded, a brief tip of the chin. Her gaze met Amanda's for a half-second before darting to the table then her lap. She wanted to sink through the floor like the Wicked Witch of the West. Just melt away, never to return.

"What did you do?" Amanda asked.

"I can't."

"Come on, Taylor. You know you'll tell me eventually now. 'Fess up." When Taylor remained silent, she added, "Save our friendship."

Taylor looked back at Amanda as a tear spilled over one eyelid and slid down her cheek. *Damn her,* she thought. *Why couldn't she leave well-enough alone?*

"I'm trying to, but you won't let me. You're going to hate me," she said. "Those tops and things weren't the only things I've stolen."

Amanda's eyes narrowed. "Oh?"

Taylor continued looking down, shame now burying the ability to meet Amanda's gaze. "Yes." She struggled with what she was about to say. "I—I can't seem to help it."

"What have you taken that would make me hate you?"

Taylor's heart hammered in her chest. Was she really going to say? Could she? The idea of telling Amanda about this was like deciding to fly a plane without any training. She wasn't sure if she would land safely or end up in a pile of the wreckage of her life. She took a deep breath and let it out, her chest trembling with the effort to keep from bursting into tears and running away.

Her head still down, she said, "Among other things, your mother's wedding and engagement rings."

Amanda gasped. Her mother had died when she was sixteen, and the rings had been Amanda's most cherished possessions. They had disappeared one day about a year ago. She'd had a small party, just a few friends were invited, and two days later, she'd noticed they were no longer where she kept them. Amanda had blamed a woman she'd recently met that was more a friend of a friend. She had even confronted the woman, which had led to an ugly scene, and until that moment, Amanda had been absolutely certain the woman had taken the rings.

She glared at Taylor. "Where are they?"

Taylor did her best to hold back her tears of shame. "I hocked them."

Amanda's fresh tears blurred the image of Taylor. She felt sick to her stomach and thought she might vomit at any moment. Taylor? Her best friend? She'd taken the rings? Amanda remembered accusing the woman. Taylor had been there, watching the woman deny it and staying silent.

Amanda felt a surge of hate that she wanted to will away but couldn't. She rose from the table and said quietly, "I never want to see or hear from you again." With that, she stormed out of Sinthia's the way she'd left the hotel earlier that day following the interview that changed her life forever. Anger and humiliation were suffocating her.

Taylor left after paying for the tea they'd ordered. She called work and said she'd become ill at lunch and wouldn't be coming back until morning at the earliest.

For days, Amanda stewed over the revelation. She remembered Taylor using the phrase, "among other things." She wondered what other things there might be. Her mind continued coming back to her former "best friend a girl ever had."

The next day, Amanda called a therapist and made arrangements to start sessions with her. She arrived for the appointment and sat in the waiting area, wondering if she would ever get over this betrayal.

"She said she couldn't help it?" Dr. Sanders asked after Amanda told her story.

Amanda looked at the woman seated in the chair beside her, the doctor was staring at her, awaiting an answer.

"Yes."

"Is she seeing a therapist?"

"I don't know. Why?"

"She might be suffering from kleptomania."

"Why would that matter? She took my mother's rings."

"Kleptomaniacs will often steal things they don't need or even want."

"She hocked the rings. She wanted money."

"Do you think it's possible that she hocked them because their presence made her feel guilty."

Amanda didn't like the direction this was taking. She was the one seeking help here. Taylor could go fuck herself for all she cared. "Why should I care?" she said, anger straining her voice.

"Because. She is your best friend in the world. Your words, not mine. You obviously still care about her. You're the one who used the present tense. If you really care, you should try to help her deal with this problem. Do you believe she hated you when she took the rings?"

"No."

"Was she angry at you at the time? Was she seeking revenge for something you did or said?"

"No, she wouldn't do that. She'd talk to me first."

"Then why don't you talk to her? She obviously knew you would be angry about this. She had to be aware you might react this way, cutting off the friendship with a quick slice. But you persisted in knowing the secret she had, and now you both are miserable about it. Of course, I can't guarantee she's feeling any misery, but I'd bet my license on it."

"Why do you keep putting this back on me? I'm the patient here, not Taylor!"

"You came to see me because you're having difficulty dealing with what happened, right?"

"Yes."

"Can you change the past?"

"Of course not."

"Then what can you change?"

"I can't change the future," Amanda whined.

"Can't you?"

Amanda stared at the doctor, numb from the wild emotions that had been assailing her since Taylor's confession.

When she didn't respond, the doctor continued. "Let's put it this way. There's only one thing you can change here, and that's how you look at what happened. Once you do that, everything else will fall into place. You won't get over this until you forgive her, even if what she did was the most horrible thing imaginable."

Amanda considered the doctor's words. Had Taylor just been following an irresistible impulse? If that's what Taylor was doing, then could she forgive her for taking and hocking the rings? She met the doctor's eyes and felt what had become a nearly constant need to cry take her once more. Only this time, she felt better after shedding the tears.

When the session ended, she left the building and climbed into her car. She took out her phone. Moments passed, then a frightened voice answered.

"Amanda?"

"I'm sorry, Hon," Amanda said through the tears. "Do you want to talk?"

HUMOR

WHAT TOMORROW BRINGS

This story originally appeared in Fiction on the Web in September 2018.

From the author: The idea for this story came from overhearing a conversation between a son and his mother at a restaurant. The son was asking his mother for money—a lot of it. She wasn't ready to give him as much as he was asking for, and they grew rather loud as the son tried to coax and then guilt-trip his mother into giving him the money. Their evening did not go like this fictional one, but last I heard, the young man was not getting the cash.

Jenny Fremont sat alone at the small table in Mama Guali's, her favorite restaurant. She and Bob had discovered the quaint Italian diner one night when a sudden rain storm had forced them to find refuge. Now here she sat once again, waiting for Bob.

She had fallen in love with the simple ambiance of Mama Guali's the moment they had dashed in from the cloudburst. Tables with just enough space between them to prevent crowding while promoting coziness dotted the dining area like small islands. Each was draped with red and white tablecloths in the cliché checkerboard pattern, while wooden chairs gathered around the tables, keeping them company until someone sat down to join the party. Colorful, net-wrapped globes of glass on each table held a lit candle and squatted beside a drinking glass offering stale bread sticks. Aromas of tomato, basil, oregano, and garlic melted from the kitchen into the dining area, making mouths water. Yes, simply being here made her smile.

Then she thought again of Bob. She could not understand how anyone could be late every single time no matter what, but that was Bob. He lived in his own time zone. She had long ago given up trying to change this bad habit. Three months into dating him she decided it was something she would either have to accept or it would ruin the relationship. She was nearing thirty, though, already twenty-eight when they met with twenty-nine just around the corner, so she chose acceptance. Her finger, however, was still without a ring. Oh, she had rings, just not *that* ring. The one she hoped to get tonight.

She looked at the door each time the tiny bell dangling above it jingled, hoping it was finally Bob. He had insisted they meet there, the restaurant they called their "special place," saying he had an important question to ask her. She could think of no other question he might ask that absolutely required they meet at this one diner, so she felt certain tonight would be the night. She was willing to forgive his many bad habits if only he would make more permanent plans. The subject of marriage had come up, just without any hint as to when he might take the next step toward matrimony. Maybe her mother had been right about that "Why buy the cow if you get the milk for free?" argument.

Ding-ding! She glanced up and was finally greeted by Bob's smiling face, his thick, dark mustache and blue eyes making her breath catch. He plopped down opposite her as if he had run from work to be there.

"Have you ordered yet?" he asked.

"No. I was waiting for you."

"Okay. Sorry to keep you waiting."

She smiled at him. In a way his tardiness was cute, almost endearing it was so reliable.

"I'm used to it by now," she chirped.

The waiter brought Bob some water as Jenny took a sip of her own.

"Bud Light," Bob told the waiter, who nodded and turned to take care of another customer nearby.

"So, how was your day?" Jenny asked.

"Oh, the usual. One woman bought a pair of pumps that, if she'd waited until tomorrow, would've cost half that."

Jenny's brow furrowed. "You didn't tell her?"

"Honey, I work on commission."

"That doesn't mean you have to gouge people."

"That's not gouging. Gouging is charging more than they're worth. The shoes are worth what she paid."

"Still," Jenny said, squinting, "it doesn't sound honest."

"Well, it is. Besides, I need the money for…something."

"Oh?" Jenny's brows shot up as she did her best not to grin.

Bob picked up the menu as if he hadn't read it a dozen times before. Mama Guali's never changed the menu. It suggested a permanence Jenny loved.

"Why do you need money?" she asked, prodding him. "Are you saving up for something special?"

"Hmm?" he asked, still studying the menu as if it were an ancient tablet of hieroglyphics.

"I said, are you saving up for something special?"

He looked at her as if he only now noticed she was there. "Oh, well, sort of. I guess it depends."

"On what?"

"As it happens, on you."

"Oh, really?" She leaned forward and conjured her most seductive tone. "It does?"

"Yes. You see, I have a question I need to ask you."

"Ask away," she said, wiggling the fingers of her left hand. "I'm all ears." She hoped her smile was as seductive as her voice.

"Well, you see," he began. The waiter stepped up with his beer, putting it on a napkin before turning away again. Lifting the beer, Bob picked up the salt shaker and salted the napkin.

"You're wasting their salt," Jenny said.

"I'm sure the cost of my beer covers it. You know I hate it when the napkin sticks to the bottom of the glass."

She sighed, doing her best to be patient. "Go on. You were saying?" she prompted.

"What?" he said, sipping his beer and leaving a foam mustache clinging to his own.

Jenny cringed. "You said you have a question for me?" She wanted to scream. The beer had ruined the moment. Now, she would always think of a beer mustache when she remembered his proposal.

"Oh," he said, clearing his throat, "well yes." He took a deep breath and let it out slowly. Then thankfully wiping his upper lip with his palm, he said, "I was wondering if you would lend me twenty-four-thousand dollars."

Jenny felt her smile falter, droop and disappear. "What?"

"Yes, I need twenty-four-thousand dollars."

Jenny lifted her left hand and stared at it. "You want me to pay for—"

"Oh, no! You won't be paying for anything. It's just a loan. I'll pay you back."

"Well, that's a relief," she said. Her voice had moved from seductive to puzzled to sarcastic in seconds. She wondered for a moment if she would get arrested if she punched him.

"Yeah, I want to make a down payment on a house."

She felt the chair back press against her shoulders as she leaned back. *Why are these chairs so damned uncomfortable?* she thought. "A house?"

"Yeah."

"Oooo-kay."

"Good. Thank you," he said, raising his beer in a silent toast.

She looked at him as if he had thrown a rock at her. "No, that wasn't an 'I'll lend you the money' okay; it was an 'I get it now' okay."

Bob's eyebrows furrowed. "Are you upset?"

"I'm sorry. It's just I've never had a guy ask me for money before."

"Jenny, I'm not just a guy."

She looked at him, wondering. "I'm not sure what you are, actually."

"I'm your boyfriend," he said.

"For now."

"What's that supposed to mean?" he asked, grabbing a bread stick and snapping a bite off.

"It means for now you're my boyfriend. Who knows what tomorrow may bring?"

"I want tomorrow to bring a house. I know you have the money. You told me about that sixty-thousand dollars your grandmother left you that's been sitting in a bank doing nothing for two years. The most expensive thing I've ever seen you buy was my birthday dinner."

"Can I help it if I'm careful with my money?"

"Careful? Frugal doesn't even approach it. You've never even come into the store to buy a pair of nice shoes from me," he said. "You buy your shoes at—Where Your Soles." His face wrinkled in disgust at the name, as if he had swallowed something awful.

"Your shoes are overpriced, so you *do* gouge your customers. Anyway, that money's my rainy-day fund."

"Rainy-day fund? That's a hurricane fund! And we live in Massachusetts!"

"Shh. You're shouting."

Bob looked around at the faces turned toward him. Blushing, he turned back to Jenny and said,

"We've been dating for over a year now. I'd think you'd trust me by now."

Jenny thought for a moment. "Only one year? I thought it was longer," she said, frowning and trying to figure out what that meant.

"I've borrowed from you before and you had no problem with it. Remember that time I forgot my wallet and you paid for dinner? I paid you back."

"That was forty dollars. This is *twenty-four-thousand*! How do I know you'd pay me back?"

"I give you my word," he said. He stared at her.

"Your *word*? You wouldn't even tell a woman she could get the same shoes for half price if she waited a day."

"That wasn't the woman I love," he said, sitting back. "Let's look at this logically. Worst case is you end up owning ten percent of a house, including land—property, Jenny—that will appreciate. If I sold it for more, you'd realize an immediate return on your investment!"

"Does it have to be an investment, Bob? What happened to the idea of maybe getting married one day? And what's wrong with your apartment?"

"It's too small," he said.

"You live alone, Bob. *Still*."

He sighed. "As this woman who's careful with her money once said, 'Who knows what tomorrow will bring?'"

"Well, it's not bringing twenty-four-thousand dollars."

"So you won't lend me the money?"

Her eyes flashed fire. "For a shoe salesman, you're pretty bright."

Sitting back, he took a deep breath and looked around. "Where's the waiter? Typical service for this joint." He took a large swallow of his beer, grabbed another bread stick, and glared at her. "Are you ready to order? I suggest you have the *crab marinara*."

Crossing her arms, she stared at him, trying to think of a retort that would fit. She considered several until the perfect one occurred to her. When it did, her mouth curved into a wicked smile. "I suggest you have the *spaghetti*." She glared at him, waiting for him to make the connection that she knew would come in time.

He stared back at her, his face questioning. She could tell he knew there was an insult in there somewhere if he could only find it. With sudden understanding, his jaw dropped. "That's below the belt, Jenny."

She continued to smile, but there was no humor in it. "Exactly. Anyway, if the shoe fits."

They sat staring at one another, like boxers looking for a weakness to exploit. The waiter approached them, his steps tentative as if he expected one or both of them to explode.

"What will you have tonight?" he began. "We have a special on—"

"She'll have the crab marinara!" Bob said, interrupting him while returning Jenny's glare.

"He'll have the spaghetti!" Jenny snapped.

"Um . . . okay," the waiter said and backed away.

"I'll be back," Bob said. He stood and marched toward the bathroom.

Jenny sat in what was becoming an increasingly uncomfortable chair, fuming. She snatched up a bread stick and took a bite. Stale. *Why can't this place change out the bread sticks once in a while?* she thought.

She felt a tap on her shoulder. Startled, she turned to see her friend Donna McGee. To Jenny, sharing the misery felt like the right thing to do, even if it was with Donna, the girl with the perfect figure, perfect hair, perfect teeth. Perfect *everything*.

"Hey, girl!" Donna said, grinning.

"Hey, yourself," Jenny said, her mood evident.

Donna frowned. "What's wrong?"

"Bob."

Donna's eyebrows twitched upward. "What about him?"

"You'll never believe what he just did!"

"What?" Donna asked, sitting in Bob's seat.

"He asked me for money."

"How much? Is he short and can't pay for dinner? Doesn't he have a credit card?"

"I could handle that," Jenny said, nearly in tears from anger and frustration. "He wants to borrow twenty-four-thousand dollars!"

Donna's jaw dropped and her eyes bulged. "Holy—really?!"

"Yes."

"What does he need that much for?"

"He needs it for a down payment on a house."

"For the two of you?"

"Not yet," Jenny said, holding up her left hand. "You see any rings there?"

"Calm down, Jenny. You aren't giving it to

79

him, are you?"

"Do I have 'stupid' tattooed on my forehead? Of course not. But what am I going to do? I never had a guy ask me for money before. At least not that much. Not even close."

"Honey, if it were me, I'd send him packing," Donna said. "Once a guy stoops to asking for money, it's all over if you ask me. The nerve of some guys!"

"Really? You think I should break up with him? I mean, it's a lot of money, but we've been dating for a year."

"That's all?" said Donna. "It seems longer than that."

Jenny frowned, still trying to decide what that meant. "Yeah, I thought so too."

"Next thing you know, he'll be asking for help with the mortgage payment." Donna's voice dropped an octave. "Honey, I'm a little short this month. Can you help out with my house payment?"

Jenny's mouth gaped. "Oh my God! You're right! He'll probably bring up that I own part of the house anyway since I doubt that he'll ever pay me back. He's already talked about that tonight when I turned him down for the loan." Jenny's panic boiled to the surface as she considered the possibilities. "He might even say I owe ten percent of the house payment every month!"

"There. See? Breaking up is too good for him!" Donna said, folding her hands over Jenny's, which now appeared to be wrestling each other.

Jenny's face flashed determination. Donna was right. Why stay with a guy like that? She was still young, after all, only twenty-nine. Why waste more time on a guy like Bob? And hadn't she been appalled that he wouldn't tell that lady about the upcoming sale? He was a cheapskate. If she lent him the money, she'd never see a dime of it. If she didn't, he would resent it forever.

"I'll do it. I'm going to break up with him as soon as he gets back."

"And no going back either. If you take him back next week, you've given him title to your principles." Donna sat back, her own anger flashing like sparks. "The nerve of that guy!"

As Bob came out of the bathroom, Donna saw him and rose. "Good luck," she said. When Bob approached the table, she said. "Hi, Bob! Enjoy!" Then turning to Jenny, she said, "Talk later, okay?"

Donna got the waiter's attention, and he seated her at a nearby table.

"Bob, we have to talk," Jenny said as he sat.

"Yes," he said, his voice calmer. "Listen, why don't you come look at the house. At least do me that favor."

"No, Bob. This is about more than the house. It's about more than the money."

"Then, what is it about?" Bob's face fell.

"Bob, I think we should . . . get fresh starts. You know, with other people."

Bob stared blankly at her. "You're breaking up with me?"

"Well…yes. I'm breaking up with you."

"Just because I asked for a loan?"

"It's more than that. We've, well, we've stagnated. I mean, look at us. We keep coming to the same lousy restaurant, and—"

"I thought you loved Mama Guali's."

"I do, or at least I did. It's sort of like I used to love you." Those words hit her as having been true for some time. "But I don't anymore." She looked at Bob. "I'm sorry."

Jenny picked up her purse, took out a compact, and checked herself in the small mirror. Standing, she said, "I have to consider my future. We're not going anywhere. My mom keeps warning me about my biological clock, and I feel it's in overdrive right now."

"But you're only thirty!" he said.

She glared at him. "I'm only twenty-nine." Turning, she walked out of what had once been her favorite restaurant without turning back.

Bob sat there, staring at the door. The tinkling of the bell over the door as Jenny left sounded like a death knell. He noticed Donna sitting beside him.

"What happened?" she asked, concern coloring her features.

"Jenny just broke up with me," he said.

"She did? What for? I mean, any girl would feel lucky to have a guy like you." Reaching out, she took his hands in hers. Her voice soothing and soft, she said, "Tell me all about it."

As he launched into his story, Donna smiled. She figured within a month she could get him to move into her spacious condo and share the rent. It would work for both of them.

ACCIDENTAL RENDEZVOUS

Author note: I wrote this story as part of a writer's retreat assignment in the mountains of North Carolina one summer years ago. The other participants liked it, and I hope you do, too. I also like the narrator of this story. Like so many of us, she is flawed but very likeable because she makes so many of the mistakes that we all make once in a while. I hope you like her, too. I even borrowed the first paragraph to start my next novel, Saving Twigs.

I love walks, especially on warm, breezy days like today when the sun is so bright it's blinding even when you don't look right at it. Mama says the sun gave me my red hair. She says one day the sun just reached right down and touched it, and it turned into the flaming red it is now. I used to actually, really believe her, but I'm too old for that now, having turned thirteen on my last birthday.

Anyway, I was just walking, you know, looking at all of Grandma's flowers in her garden that stretches, like, forever. Mostly I was minding my own business, though I have to admit I was thinking a lot about how silly it was that Carla Denning, my best friend, was actually, really writing letters to Justin Timberlake and asking if she could maybe marry him when she turned eighteen. How silly! I mean, everyone knows Justin

Timberlake is yesterday's news. If I were Carla, I'd be writing Johnny Depp.

Well, anyway, I was walking through Grandma's garden when suddenly, right out of nowhere, there's this man lying in the grass. I mean, he's just *lying* there, using a small backpack like a pillow as if he had some business being in my grandma's garden.

At first, I thought he was dead, and to be honest I was kind of hoping he was. Not that I'm morbid or anything or even that I thought he might hurt me if he was alive. It's just that if he was actually, really dead, then there would be at least *some* excitement to give me some relief from my boring existence.

"Hello," he said. Shucks! He was alive.

"Hi," I answered, as if I came upon men lying in the grass in my grandmother's garden every day.

"I guess you're wondering what I'm doing here."

"Not particularly," I lied. "It's a free country." And that wasn't a lie, at least for everyone but me.

He must have known I was lying, though, because he told me why he was here anyway. "I was walking along the road over there," he said, pointing into the distance where the road ran by my grandma's property, "and it looked so lovely I thought I should lie down and look at the blue sky."

He could tell how ridiculous that sounded. Either that or my patented "don't kid a kidder" look clued him in to how completely insane his reason was.

"No, really. It's true. Haven't you ever felt like there was something you *had* to do, no matter what?"

Well, I had, but I wasn't admitting it to him, so I said, "No." I was getting good at this lying thing. Maybe it was because he didn't know me the way Mama did. She could see a lie coming before I drew a breath to tell it.

"You know that's not true," he said matter-of-factly and smiled.

Dang! Was there some kind of radar adults had that told them when kids were lying? I mean, that was *two* lies he had seen through already. It was actually, really disconcerting.

(*Disconcerting* is my word of the day. I'm working on improving my vocabulary, and I read in *Y M* that learning and using a new word every day was a good way to go.)

Anyway, I frowned at him and my curiosity took over. "Who are you, anyway?"

"My name's Justin," he said, sitting up so he could look like a normal person.

"Justin, huh?" Carla would be impressed. Of course, he didn't look anything like Justin Timberlake, but Carla was easily impressed so that didn't matter.

"And you are—a?" He let the question hang in the air like a fill-in-the-blank, while I stood there feeling like a ninny for not offering my name. I was sure he thought I was about the rudest person on the planet.

"I'm Carla." Another lie of course, and this one

got through his radar, but I wasn't going to tell him my real name was Maureen, which I loathed (a former word of the day). He might start calling me "Mo" for short the way Mama always did, which actually, really made me feel like that one guy with the weird haircut in the Three Stooges, which for some reason my dad loved to watch when they came on one of those TV for old people channels. The absolute *horror* of that name! Every year at school I tried to get the teachers to call me "Starr," but they refused. And the worst part was that I didn't even have a middle name to fall back on.

"Are you there? Hello?!"

He'd been talking and my mind was blathering away to whoever it blathered away to when I talk to myself, which is a lot.

"Sorry. My mind wanders sometimes." I could tell by the look on his face that *that* one rang true on his radar.

"That's okay, Carla. Mine does too, sometimes."

Carla? Puzzled, I looked around, thinking she was approaching behind me and wondering at the same time how he knew her. Then I remembered. Dang! This could get confusing, so I changed the subject with an excuse.

"Well, it was just disconcerting coming up on you like that. I thought you were dead or something." I noticed a slight upward twitch of his eyebrows at my use of the word *disconcerting* and proudly smiled inside because my efforts at self-improvement were working.

"As you can see, I'm quite alive." He stood up.

That's when I noticed some things about him. Like I noticed he wasn't as old as I thought. At first, I thought he was old, like over thirty, but now I could see he was maybe only about twenty-three or so. Next, I noticed he was tall, like five-ten. I'm five-five-and-an-eighth, and I just could never be with any guy not taller than me. Not that I thought about Justin and me, like, *being* together, but you know what I mean. But I must admit the third thing I noticed about him was that he was gorgeous. I thought it was funny how I hadn't noticed it before, but I chalked that up to him being below me on the ground and seeming short that way. I remember thinking that he looked a lot like Johnny Depp, except that his eyes and nose were different, and his mouth was narrower and his chin was wider.

I suddenly felt dizzy. My heart was trying to pound its way out of my chest, my mouth went dry, and my knees turned rubbery. It was love at first sight, or at least second sight. *I'm actually, really in love*, I thought to myself. I always knew it would happen one day, but I had never expected this.

Then something wonderful-terrible happened. That dizziness got worse—like a lot! The next thing I knew I had fainted—actually, really fainted—well sort of, and was on the ground myself and he was kneeling over me and looking all concerned-like. His gorgeous eyebrows were all knitted together so much that they looked like a caterpillar had crawled onto his face, which was kind of strange looking. He was brushing the hair out of my face and saying, "Carla, are you all right?"

"Where's Carla?" I was in a stupor (see how

this word thing works?) and had totally forgotten my lie—again.

Then he looked actually, really weird, as if he was suddenly scared or something. "You're Carla. Don't you remember your name?"

"Oh…yeah," I blinked and tried to sit up, turning redder than my hair.

"You might want to stay down there and let the blood and oxygen get back to your head. That will help stop the dizziness."

He sat beside me in the grass and I lay back feeling a bit weird with him above me like that and me lying in the grass as he had done before. Then I began to wonder, what if he tries to kiss me? That kind of scared me. I mean, what *if* he tried to kiss me? Where would my nose go? Would it get in the way? It was awfully big, and it had a habit of making itself known at the worst times, like when I sneezed *very* suddenly and without warning last Thanksgiving *all over* the turkey. You couldn't really see anything gross, if you know what I mean, but everyone knew I had sneezed on it, so of course, nobody wanted any. I won't go into details except to say the dog got a lot more turkey last Thanksgiving than we did.

So I began to wonder what I would do with my nose if he leaned in for a kiss. It would surely get in the way. I mean, it *was* my nose, a honker if there ever was one. So of course, thinking about that made my nose itch like crazy.

I needed to rub my nose, but Justin was looking at me. Not *looking* looking, just, well, you know, he could see me, and I didn't want to rub my nose because that can be kind of disgusting. So I pointed at the sky and said, "What kind of bird is that?"

His radar apparently on the fritz, he looked up to where I was pointing at the empty, blue sky. When he did, I quickly used my other hand to rub my nose really hard for a second, trying to make the sneezy feeling go away. Well, sometimes that helps and sometimes it makes things worse. You can guess which one happened this time.

He continued looking at the sky, searching for the bird that was never there, and I was starting to feel all panicky, what with my sneeze coming on like one of those Japanese trains that goes like two-hundred-miles-an-hour.

It's a funny thing about sneezes. Some people sneeze real dainty and quiet, but not me. Let me tell you about my sneezes, just so you can get the idea how bad they are. There was this tree near my house, and its branches all pointed as straight up as they could toward the sky. One winter the leaves had fallen off the branches, and my older sister said that I had sneezed on the tree to make it that way. I mean, *that* is how big my sneezes are. I only know that if that stuff is inherited from someone in the family, I want that person eliminated from my family's gene pool.

Anyway, Justin was looking up at the sky and my nose was about to explode.

So, of course, it did.

It was one of those atom bomb sneezes that make your nose feel like it may have come off. I quickly covered my nose and cheeks with my hands and looked up at Justin to see the very startled look on his face, the ghost bird apparently forgotten.

Needless to say, my earnest prayer for the earth to please open up and swallow me whole, never to be seen again, was as big a failure as this encounter with Justin was turning out to be.

"You must think I'm gross!" I said through my cupped hands. Always the gentleman, it seemed, he reached into his backpack and handed me a hankie, which he was kind enough to let me keep as a souvenir.

"Not really. You just sneezed. Everyone does, you know."

"Not like that! My sister says my sneezes are like gas explosions or even atom bombs."

"I wouldn't go that far. I'd say your sneeze has character."

Was he crazy? I'd just nearly sneezed my nose right off my face. Character? I had to ask. "What do you mean, character?"

"Well, you know. It's—unique."

Yeah, unique like volcanic eruptions, I thought. "Carla says my sneezes are like the eruption of Mount St. Helens. Big and loud with lots of fallout."

He looked at me, puzzled. "There's another Carla?" After a moment's thought about my complete failure to remember the lie, I decided to come clean with him.

Looking away from his mesmerizing gaze, I mumbled that Carla wasn't my real name and told him how it was the name of my best friend.

"Oh, I see. That explains some things."

"Are you mad at me for lying?"

"No. For one thing, you don't know me. I can understand if you don't give me your name. For another, I wasn't totally honest myself."

I think my jaw dropped. Apparently, my own radar was totally not working or something. Maybe it doesn't develop until you're older, I thought.

"What did you lie about?"

My imagination began to run wild. Instantly, I saw him saying things like, 'I lied when I said I didn't love you,' but of course he'd never said that anyway. At that particular fantasy, I began to come to my senses and realized our age differences and how he could never actually, really love me, even if we could become friends, which was surely doubtful because of that age thing.

Again, my mind had been blathering on and I missed what he said.

"What?"

"I said I lied when I told you why I was lying in the grass."

"Why were you?"

He paused for a moment, seeming to make a decision, I guess whether or not to come clean with me, but his response was not very mysterious, which of course disappointed me. "I'm on a walking tour of the area and slept in the grass last night. I didn't want you to get alarmed and think I was a criminal who was hiding from the police or something."

I told him that would actually, really have been better than just the walking thing. At least then my life would have had some excitement.

"You mean coming upon a strange man

sleeping in the grass wasn't exciting?"

I thought about that for a minute. "I guess it was. Thanks," I said, smiling broadly. "But it would have been better if you'd been a criminal," I added with a grin.

He shrugged. "Sorry to disappoint you."

"That's okay. My mom would have a fit if I stopped to talk to a criminal. But Carla would certainly be impressed."

We said good-bye and he began walking to the road in the distance. The garden was lit up by the crawling sun and more colorful than I remembered it ever being before. He waved wordlessly and walked out of my life as quickly as he'd come into it. Just like that.

I began to wonder if he had been actually, really truthful about who he was. Maybe he *had* been a criminal but just hadn't admitted it. I mean, I know I wouldn't admit it to some strange person I had met in a garden where I wasn't supposed to be in the first place.

My imagination began to work away again, making my dreary life more exciting. Suddenly, he was a criminal on the lam. A killer maybe. That had to be it. He was a killer of young girls running from the cops, and he'd decided to leave me alive to wonder about it.

Then I began to wonder *why* he let me live. He certainly could have killed me and probably gotten away. Then it hit me. Maybe he actually, really liked me. He may have even loved me. My mind spun further into the fantasy. I was now a wanted criminal's girlfriend. A moll, I think they used to call them. I would contact him and tell him he could hide in our basement, or something, where we would be lovers and plan his escape.

Finally, though, I gave that part of the fantasy up because Mama said my imagination sometimes went into overdrive to the point that I sometimes had trouble distinguishing between what was real and what wasn't. But then, what does she know?

In my mind, though, I held onto my little daydream and still wondered why he didn't kill me, thinking how he sure was polite about it and all. I finally concluded I was one of the lucky ones.

I turned and went back to Grandma's, deciding not to mention it to my mom. She wouldn't believe me anyway, even if I showed her the hankie Justin let me keep. But it was better that way, I guess. A girl has to have her secrets, you know. Anyway, the look on Carla's face when I told her would be worth it all, even the embarrassment of the sneeze.

Suddenly, I couldn't wait to see Carla in school Monday. Boy, would I have a story for her about how I had met this man named Justin (she'd *love* that) who probably had liked me in spite of our age difference, and how maybe he'd been a criminal on the run.

Yes, life was no longer boring thanks to Justin. Not at all.

HAIR TODAY, GONE TOMORROW

Author's note: I wrote the first version of this story many years ago at a time when unusual hair colors were not a fashion statement but a reason for ridicule or worse. That is no longer the case, but I like this story, so I am including it in this collection. Otherwise, nobody would ever see it because the problem is no longer a problem, and that would be a shame. So, dear reader, turn back the clocks in your heads to a time when the only acceptable hair colors fell within the framework of brunette, blonde, or redhead.

Rita sat on the bed and worried. She didn't really know what to do, and the thought *What will Ted think?* kept running through her mind like one child tormenting another. She stood up and went to the mirror at her dresser, sat, and stared at the catastrophe.

Green. Her hair was green for God's sake. Not just a green tint or something. Green, like a field of grass. In fact, that was what it looked like. A bunch of grass. She'd wanted to surprise Ted by greeting him at the door as a blonde. She knew he liked blondes. God knows she had to put up with his stupid, misogynistic growls when they spent time at the beach last summer whenever a sexy little thing in a bikini walked by with her blonde tresses falling down her back toward her cute little ass. Rita was

94

only twenty-four, and not that bad looking herself, and Ted's constant leering at blondes had pissed her off. What was wrong with her ass? Wasn't it cute?

So she had decided to color her hair blonde. Her mistake, of course, was using an off-brand she'd never heard of. She should have gone with something more expensive, but they were saving every penny they could to redecorate the study as a nursery. She wasn't pregnant yet—never would be with that damn green hair—but they were planning on it. Or they had been. She wondered if Ted would take one look at her and decide never to touch her again. She considered shaving her head, causing more tears to spill.

Then the sound of the apartment door opening shocked her into action. She grabbed the paper bag that the dye and the few other items she'd bought at the store had been in, ran to turn off the bedroom lights, and sat back on the bed before putting the bag over her head.

Seconds ticked by. Then minutes. Was it Ted out there? Or had fate decided to really mess with her and they were being burglarized? She was about to get up to see, figuring a burglar would take one look at the woman with green hair and run, when the bedroom door creaked and light spilled in from the living room.

Ted stuck his head around the edge of the door, trying to see in the darkness. For the thousandth time, Ted wanted to strangle the idiots who had designed this tiny apartment and put the light switch on the other side of the door forcing them to walk around the opened door to switch them on. Ted was stuck peering into darkness.

"Rita? You in here?"

"No," she said, knowing she had to answer just as she would eventually have to show him the long grass on her head, just not yet if she could help it.

"Rita, don't joke around. I can't see you at all. Why's it so dark?"

"Because I want it dark."

"What's that about? Here, let me turn on the light. It's spooky with you sitting in here in the dark."

"I don't want the lights on! I just want to sit here in the dark."

Ted was more than confused. Usually, Rita met him at the door, kissing him hello as if she'd been waiting for him to come home and nothing else. It wasn't the *here, honey, here's your drink, why don't you sit down while I make dinner* kind of greeting. She was much too independent for that. But it was definitely one of the things he looked forward to at the end of a day of doing his best to convince people the furniture he was selling was worth the price the store was asking. Never an easy task, mostly because it wasn't true.

So when he'd arrived home to what felt like an empty apartment, he'd gotten spooked. He thought maybe she was downstairs finishing the laundry in the building's laundry room, so he'd sat for a few minutes, waiting for her to come in. Then he wondered if she was in their bedroom or the adjoining bath and had opened the door to find the room dark and his wife sitting in the dark room.

It was unnerving, to say the least.

96

He peered into the darkness toward Rita's voice coming from the bed. He could see from her shadow that she was sitting there, but something appeared to be on her head.

"Let me just turn on the lights, Rita. I can't see."

"Ted, you touch those lights, and I swear, I'll file for divorce."

"What? Don't be ridiculous."

"Okay, maybe you'll file for divorce. I just don't want the lights on."

Ted decided enough was enough and went to the light switch, flipping it on. "Ah, finally. Let there be light." He turned to his wife on the bed.

"Rita?"

"Yes?"

"Why is there a paper sack over your head?"

"Go away! I don't want you to see me like this."

"You don't want me to see you with a paper bag over your head?"

"No, I don't want you to see me with what's under the paper bag."

"Did you cut yourself? Did you get stitches? What is it?" He was starting to worry. Rita wasn't acting like herself. Not at all.

"Nothing. I'll let you see eventually, but I have to get used to the idea."

Ted walked to the bed and sat beside her. "Don't be silly." He reached for the bag and started to lift it, but Rita's hands shot out and clamped the bag down on her head, her arms folded over it to prevent him from removing it.

"Okay, you're freaking me out here, Rita. What the hell is going on?"

"Just let me show you in my own time. Please?"

Ted looked around and said, "Okay. Fine. Have it your way. I'll be out in the living room wondering what I can fix myself for dinner."

He stood and walked to the door. As he opened it, he slipped his shoes off before closing it. Then holding his shoes, he tiptoed quickly to the other side of the bed and crouched down. He watched as Rita slowly lifted the paper bag above her eyes so she could see.

Glancing around the room and feeling safe, she removed the bag entirely.

"Oh, my God!" Ted exclaimed.

Rita turned. "Ted! You tricked me!"

"What did you expect? You refused to tell me." He stared at her hair. "What the hell happened to your hair?"

"I dyed it."

"You dyed it? But it's—it's—green."

"Oh, really? I hadn't noticed." She glared at her husband, suddenly wondering why she had tried to please him with a new hair color in the first place.

"Well, I mean, why did you dye it green?"

"Haven't you heard? It's the latest in spring fashion. Doesn't it remind you of spring?"

"There's no reason to be sarcastic."

"Ted! My hair is green! Do you know of a better time for sarcasm?"

"So you didn't mean to color it green?"

"Wow, you are definitely sharp today."

Ted ignored her response, approaching the problem logically instead. "Okay, Rita. Calm down a bit. Let's consider this. What happened?"

"I wanted to change my hair color to blonde for you. I bought this hair dye called Beached Blonde. It was a cheap off-brand because hair dye can be kind of expensive, but I wanted to surprise you."

"Well, you did that."

"Don't interrupt."

"Okay, just one more. What made you think I wanted you to be a blonde?"

"Oh, I don't know. Maybe how you would give that lusty growl at the beach every time some blonde hottie walked by?"

"Oh. I guess you didn't appreciate that."

"Like I said, you're really quick on the uptake today, aren't you?"

"Sorry."

"Well, anyway, I dyed my hair with this crap, followed all the instructions to a T because I knew sometimes dyeing your hair can come out a little differently than you expected."

Ted chuckled. "I'll say."

Rita set her jaw and glared at him, daring him to make another joke. When she knew he understood, she continued, "Anyway, when I rinsed it out, it was this color."

"Have you called the company that made the dye? Maybe they could help."

"I did," Rita said, "but I got one of those automated responses. You know, 'if you need to speak to bookkeeping, press five,' stuff like that. But they didn't have a choice for 'if our product turned your hair green, press seven."

"But you held on, right? Waited for an operator?"

"Of course, I did. She put me on hold and said someone would be with me in a minute. After thirty minutes of holding for a minute, I hung up."

"Well, what are you going to do? You work tomorrow, and you can't go in with a bag on your head. And you can't go to work with—green hair. You work for one of the most conservative law offices in the city."

"Mom is going to be here soon. She's going to help me dye it again."

Ted sat up straight. "Of course! Why didn't I think of that? Just re-dye it!"

"Ted, every time you dye your hair, it damages it. It can be playing with fire to dye it twice in one day."

"Well, you can't very well go on looking like a...well, this. It's the only thing to do, don't you think?"

At that moment their apartment buzzer sounded. Rita's mother, Doris, needed to be let into the building. "There's Mom now," Rita said. "I just asked her to come over without explaining. All she knows is saying 'no' wasn't an option. Could you, well, prepare her a little?"

Ted stood and stepped to the door. "Sure, hon. And I'll order pizza. Maybe your mom could join us." He left the room and Rita sat there. She figured it could have gone worse with Ted. He could have offered to help her shave her head.

Ted buzzed his mother-in-law in and opened

the apartment door. When she stepped through the doorway, he spread his arms and gestured to the tiny living room. "Welcome to Hell, Doris!"

She pinched her brow at him. "What's happened?" she asked as she closed the door.

For Rita, the minutes crawled by as she waited for her mother to come into the bedroom. She couldn't hear what Ted was saying, but she heard her mom say, "Oh, my God!" Then the bedroom door opened, and her mother stood there. Rita hoped she could get through this without strangling someone, possibly her mother.

"Oh, Ted. You're right. She does look like a Smurf."

"TED!" Rita wanted to punch him. "You think I look like a Smurf?!"

"Well, one of the cute ones," he answered.

"You ass!" Rita said.

Her mother intervened. "Calm down, Rita. You're the one who bought the cheap hair dye."

"Well, you both don't have to rub it in."

"Why were you dyeing your hair, anyway?" Doris asked. "You have beautiful hair. Or you did."

"I wanted to surprise Ted by being a blonde when he got home." She scowled at Ted. "Instead, he found a Smurf!"

Doris nodded, understanding. "So I take it you're ovulating."

"Mom!"

"Jeez, Rita, it's not as if I didn't do stuff like that too when I was trying to get your father's attention."

"Too much information, Mom! Can we just do

something about my hair?"

"Sure, honey. We can have that fixed in a jiffy." Doris turned to Ted. "You order the pizza and we'll be in the bathroom. I'll come get ours when it arrives. You're to stay out."

"Yes, ma'am," Ted answered, saluting her.

"Don't press your luck," Doris answered, and Ted retreated to the living room.

The pizza arrived and he called to Doris to come get theirs. Ted watched the Yankees and imagined what it would be like to be sitting in the bullpen, a member of his favorite team. It would beat selling cheap furniture for inflated prices, not to mention the difference in pay. They would be able to afford an apartment with the light switch on the correct side.

He heard a scream from their bathroom but decided it might be best to remain where he was. Going in would feel too much like stopping to stare at a car accident.

Rita stared at her reflection in the mirror. Her face, now framed with wet, cobalt blue hair, gazed back. "Oh, my God," she said, her voice a panicked squeak. "What will Ted say?"

Doris stood behind Rita, her face an etching of bewilderment. "That you still look like a cute Smurf?"

"It's not funny, Mom! Does this look funny to you?"

Doris's mouth popped open in surprise. Rita saw the sudden change in the mirror and wondered what had occurred to her mom. "What?" she said, hoping her mom had a real solution.

"Do you have any bleach?"

"Bleach? You mean you're going to really bleach my hair? I heard that wasn't good for it."

"And constant dyeing is?"

"Well, I guess you've got a point. It's under the sink in the kitchen."

Doris walked through the living room toward the kitchen, and Ted asked, "So how's it going in there?"

"Smurf-errific."

Ted watched in silence as Doris came back through the room with the bottle of bleach. Neither spoke as the bedroom door closed behind her.

Ted's interest in the ballgame waned—it was 9-1 Orioles—and he considered Rita's reaction to his playful growls at the women on the beach last summer. The more he thought about it, the worse he felt. Rita was very attractive, but she had to watch what she ate. She ran in the park on her days off, and he thought about the sacrifices she made to keep herself attractive to him.

He looked down at himself. He'd gained about ten pounds since they got married two years ago. Not a lot, but enough to say he had decided that he didn't have to really work at it anymore.

He glanced at the pizza box, the last, partially eaten piece of pepperoni pizza accusing him. He'd ordered extra cheese as well. He wondered how many calories he'd just consumed and decided they were too many. He wanted to go throw it all back up, but while he wouldn't do that, there was something he could do. It was time to start being

103

more like Rita when it came to making sure he looked good for her.

Taking out his phone, he checked his schedule for tomorrow. There would be time to go running after work. If Rita could turn her hair green for him, the least he could do was to get off his butt and try to look better for her.

Another hour passed. When the next scream issued from the bathroom, he could no longer sit passively. As Ted entered the bedroom, a shocked Rita was walking out of the bathroom like a zombie in a low-budget film.

He stared, mouth agape, at his wife's bald head.

She glared at him. "Don't you say a word! Not one damn word!"

Doris stood in the bathroom doorway, her face a study in shock.

Rita went to her vanity and sat, staring into the mirror as if looking at her bald head would make it suddenly grow blonde hair down her back.

"I look like Patrick Stewart from that old Star Trek show on TV."

"No, you don't," Doris said. "You're a lot younger than he is. You look more like Sinead O'Connor."

"Either way, I'm bald, Mom. I'm freaking bald."

"It's not bad," Ted offered.

"I look like I've got cancer."

"That's it!" Doris nearly shouted, startling Ted and Rita.

"What's it?" Rita asked.

"My friend Carol, a lady I work with. She had

cancer."

"I'm not sure what's so good about that," Rita offered.

"She has a wig."

"But isn't she using it?" Rita asked.

"Not anymore. She finished her chemo months ago. Her hair is grown out again. I bet she'd let you borrow it!"

"What color is it?"

"Oh, come now, Rita. Beggars can't be choosers."

Rita looked back to the mirror. "That's me. A bald beggar."

"If you must know, it's brown."

"Brown? That's my natural color!"

"I repeat. Beggars can't be choosers. I'll call her right now and go get it for you tonight. I'm sure she won't mind." With that, Doris bustled out the door and was gone.

Ted continued staring at Rita. She'd gone through Hell today, and all because she thought he'd lost interest, or would be more interested if she changed her hair color.

Sitting on the bed, he patted the mattress beside himself. "Come here."

"I'm not in the mood, Ted."

"I am."

She looked over at him. His leer was almost disturbing. "What?"

"So sue me. I never thought I'd think bald was so—sexy—but I do."

Rita smiled for the first time that night. "Really?"

105

"Really."

"You're not just saying that to make me feel better?"

"Nope." He continued leering at her, and she began to believe him.

She stood and dropped the towel from around her shoulders. She was topless. Ted growled. Rita was more in the mood than she had thought. "Mom's right. I'm ovulating, you know."

Holding out his arms, he said, "Then let's make a baby." She stepped toward him, her smile beaming. "A bald one," he added. "But first, call your mom and tell her you'll pick up the wig on your way to work in the morning."

After she did that, she looked at Ted. "Now, where were we?" she asked as she fell onto the bed, pushing him onto his back.

THE EMPTY CARPORT

The following story, written years ago, was converted and combined into the plot of my first novel, Floating Twigs. *It is loosely based on a real incident involving one of my aunts and her missing car, which was eventually found in basically the same place the fictional Thelma Henderson's was. I'd say more, but I don't want to give away the punch line to anyone who hasn't read* Floating Twigs.

Thelma Henderson stepped outside her small frame house and pulled hard on the door that swelled when it rained or was too humid. She turned to the empty carport with her keys ready to unlock and start the car that had simply vanished. She looked around vacantly, as if the car might have moved itself to a part of the yard to wait for her today, and blinked when it didn't appear. Yes, the car was gone, but where?

Her mind searched for answers. Who would want to steal her car? It was nearly ten years old— no, eleven—and was far from a collector's item. Worthless to everyone but her. You couldn't even get a fair price for it as a trade-in at the local Ford dealer.

Her mind ricocheted to her youth when she had decided to sleep in the top bunk when her sister had slept at a friend's. She had awakened in the night and needed to go pee when she became groggily aware that the floor had disappeared. She could distinctly recall wondering where the floor had gone as her feet met air instead of the aged, cracking wood of the bedroom floor. The feeling was just like this one, a vague wondering that did not fit her idea of reality. Indeed, the thought that her car was missing felt as strange now as the missing floor had been to her sleepy, nine-year-old mind. There was a sort of impossibility to it all.

She grabbed blindly at the first solution to this puzzle but dismissed it just as quickly. George knew it was Wednesday, the day she always went to see Frieda, her hairdresser. No way George would borrow her car. Anyway, George had his own car, and he couldn't drive two of them. Then she wondered if George was playing a trick on her. No. He knew there would be Hell to pay for such a joke, and George wasn't much of a practical joker anyway.

Still, the car was plainly gone and she had no idea where it had disappeared to.

Unlocking the old door knob to her back door and pushing against the scrape of wood against wood, she entered the house, plopped her purse down on the small, Formica-covered breakfast bar, and picked up the phone with a perturbed huff, sounding like a locomotive coming to an unscheduled stop. Her first call was to Frieda. Nora, one of the other women at the salon who pretended to be as good as Frieda at coloring and setting hair, listened intently as Thelma told her how someone had stolen her car.

"The Taurus?" Nora asked, the disbelief rising in her voice.

"Yes, the Taurus. I know what you're thinking, and the same thought occurred to me. Why in the world would anyone steal my old clunker? Well, I can't answer that. I just know it's gone."

"Must have been someone really desperate for a car," Nora said. "Maybe someone escaped from the jail or something and yours looked like an easy mark."

Just like Nora to use words like mark that she'd heard on TV, Thelma thought. Next, she'll be thinking she's better at solving crimes than the FBI.

Thelma could hear Frieda in the background ask what was wrong. The muffled sound of Nora's hand loosely covering the mouthpiece of the salon phone was followed by a hollow-sounding, "Some criminals snuck into the Henderson's carport and stole Thelma's Taurus last night!"

A brief conversation that did not include Thelma ensued until Nora remembered she had Thelma on the phone. "You should call the police," she told her.

"I would if you'd let me finish this call first. Tell Frieda I can't make it today and see if she can work me in sometime in the next few days."

"I could always—" Nora began, but Thelma cut her off.

"No, thank you, Nora Dinwiddy. I'll stick with Frieda if you don't mind. Now, good-bye," she said, hanging up before Nora could reply.

Thelma dialed 9-1-1 and waited for the answer.

"9-1-1. What's your emergency?" came Shirley Caldwell's voice. Thelma knew Shirley well; she and Thelma's daughter had gone to school together.

"Shirley? This is Thelma Henderson. My car's been stolen right out of my carport."

"Are you sure?" Shirley asked, not aware of how stupid the question sounded.

"Shirley, I'm fifty-seven years old, and that's old enough to know when my car isn't where it ought to be. Of course, unless you think I went blind or something. I got up and went out to go to my Wednesday appointment with Frieda and it was gone. Vanished."

"Well, Mrs. Henderson, 9-1-1 is only for emergencies. You'll have to call the police department number."

Reaching the limit of her patience while she wondered what other emergencies might crop up in the little town of Fairville, Thelma hung up on Shirley after getting the number from her and dialed it.

"Fairville PD, Assistant Chief Thorton speaking."

Just like Brody Thorton to announce his position like that, she thought. "Brody, this is taxpaying citizen Thelma Henderson. Is Chief Simms there?"

"Well, he is, but he's indisposed right now."

"Indisposed?" She had no idea what he meant.

"Well, Ms. Henderson, he's on the toilet."

"Why didn't you say so, instead of all that 'indisposed' garbage. I've been to the bathroom a few times myself, you know."

"Yes ma'am," he said. "Is there something I could help you with?"

"Just tell Chief Simms to come out to my place. My car's been stolen."

"Are you sure?"

What was with some people? Did they think she was senile? "No, Brody Thorton. I just thought it would be great to file a false police report and get the immense joy of paying a fine. Of course, I'm sure. It's not like it's so tiny it could hide in the grass or something, you know." She took a breath before adding, "And I'm sure as hell not senile."

"No, ma'am. Didn't say you were."

"You suggested it," she said, growing angrier by the second. "Will you just tell Harold to come out to my place as soon as he's off the crapper?"

"Yes, ma'am. I'll make sure he gets the message as soon as he comes out."

"Thank you," Thelma said. "You can go back to your game of solitaire now."

After she hung up, she waited for Police Chief Vernon Simms to come along to investigate. She knew he wouldn't leave a crime of this magnitude to either of the two officers who served under him, especially that idiot Brody Thorton, who was unbelievably second in command. In Fairville a stolen car would constitute a major crime wave. Sometimes, the town reminded her of the fictional Mayberry, it was so quiet, and the idea of an honest-to-goodness crime would certainly bring the top brass.

Fifteen minutes later, Chief Simms pulled the patrol car into the driveway and climbed out, looking around much as Thelma had, as if the car might be hiding somewhere.

Thelma knew Vernon never turned down coffee, so she'd made a pot while waiting for him. After he sat down and sipped the hot coffee with a slurpy hiss, he got to work.

"So, Mrs. Henderson," he began, using the formal mode of addressing the victim even though he'd known her all his life. "When did you notice your car was missing?"

"When I went out to start it."

"No, ma'am. I mean about what time was it?"

"Oh. It was about 9:30, I guess. I had an appointment with Frieda at ten and I had to stop at the post office on the way downtown to buy stamps, so I left early. You don't want to keep Frieda waiting or she'll move on and you'll never get in to see her."

"Had Mr. Henderson already left for the day?" Slurp.

"Yes. He'll be gone for several days on a business trip. And Vernon?"

"Yes, ma'am?"

"Cut it with the Mr. and Mrs. Henderson. You sound like we're a couple of strangers."

"Oh, okay. So, George had already left when you went out and discovered your car missing?"

"Yes."

"I see," the chief said, as if he really did. "Any chance he took your car?"

"None whatsoever. He can't drive two cars, Vernon," she said admonishingly, not admitting to herself she'd thought about it for a second herself.

Vernon slurped more coffee to cover his mistake.

"I guess you're right."

"Anyway," she went on, "if he'd taken mine, his would be in the driveway, though I wouldn't be able to drive it since I don't have a key since it's a company car. Besides that, if he'd taken my car, it would mean his wouldn't start."

Vernon nodded as if he were thinking, though Thelma knew he had no idea how to proceed. The biggest crimes in Fairville were the occasional kid shoplifting a candy bar or one of the residents getting drunk and driving somewhere, usually for more to drink. She knew deep down that unless the car showed up on its own somehow, he would probably never recover it. Too bad, too.

"It was a green Ford Taurus, wasn't it?" he finally asked.

"Yes. A dark green, like grass in the shade."

"Sorta old, wasn't it?"

Thelma sighed and told him the year of the car.

Chief Simms sipped more coffee, not slurping this time since it had cooled. A sudden thought occurred to him.

"Do you know the license number of the car?"

Thelma fished the information out of her purse. "I keep it in my purse. I never knew why until today."

She pulled out a photocopy of the car's registration that she kept in her purse and let him copy down the information he needed. She noticed he even copied down the car's weight, as if that might help find it.

After finishing his cup of coffee, Chief Simms

stood and looked as reassuring as he could. "We'll find it, Thelma. Don't you worry."

"I'm not so much worried as I'm mad. It's hard to get appointments with Frieda if you don't keep your standing one. She's harder to get in to see than a dentist."

After Vernon left, she called Frieda back to try to get another appointment, and this time Frieda answered.

"Frieda? Thelma. Listen, I'm sorry I had to cancel."

"No worry, honey. I'm just glad you weren't in it when those thugs took it."

"Hmph! If I had been, they wouldn't have taken it far, I can tell you. I'm pretty good with an umbrella, and I keep one in the back seat of the car in case it rains. So, anyway, I was calling to see if I could get in to see you on Saturday.

"Oh, honey, I'm sorry. I'm all booked up. Why Saturday?"

"George's not going to be back until then at the soonest, and he'll need to drive me there."

"Oh, well, no. I just don't have a place to fit you in, but I'm happy to hold next week's appointment for you."

"Thank you," Thelma said.

"You know, Nora could take you Saturday."

"No offence, Frieda, but I wouldn't let Nora trim my eyebrows."

Thelma hung up, hoping her words would make Frieda rethink allowing Frieda to work for her just because she was her sister-in-law. The woman cut hair like an axe murderer.

The next day, Chief Simms stopped by Thelma's. When Thelma answered the doorbell, her first words were, "You mean you found it?"

"No, Thelma. Not yet, but I will. Got any coffee?"

"Sure," she said, sighing and stepping back to let him enter.

As he sipped his coffee, he said, "I must admit that we're not used to dealing with stolen cars, Thelma. With that in mind, I called a friend who's a cop in Atlanta for some advice. He gave me a list of questions to ask. You mind answering them?"

"I guess if it will help find my car, I will."

"Okay, when did you last use your car?"

"Let's see. It was Sunday, I think. I went to church that morning by myself because George had to be somewhere on business that day."

"He works on Sundays?"

"Not often but once in a while, yes, and he'd worked that day."

"And you attend St. Paul's Episcopal, right?"

"Yes. You know that, Vernon. I was raised in that church just like you were raised a Baptist."

Vernon seemed to ignore the comment. "Then you came straight home?"

"Well, no. I went to have lunch with Amanda Collier. I met her at Craig's Cafe."

"The diner on Orchard?"

"You know another one?" she asked. She was tiring of these stupid questions.

"Did you notice anyone following you?"

"No."

"What about in Craig's? Were there any

115

strangers in there? Anyone suspicious?"

"Not that I noticed. Why are you asking me these things? If I knew who'd taken my car, I would have told you yesterday."

"Just trying to get a handle on a few things. Just bear with me. We'll be done here soon."

She sat staring at him as he consulted his small notebook. She heaved a sigh as she waited for him to decide he had enough information about her habits.

"So, then, you haven't seen the car since you got home from Craig's on Sunday afternoon?"

"Well, I didn't say that, did I? The last time I saw it was—" She stopped.

"Yes?" Vernon said, waiting for her to respond.

"Oh, my."

"Thelma?"

"Oh, dear."

"What is it? Do you remember who might have taken it?"

She looked at him, blushing a deep crimson. "Well, I guess you could say that." She began fiddling with the pearls that draped her neck.

"Thelma?" he said again, prompting her.

She looked at him and opened her mouth to speak, but instead something occurred to her and she began laughing instead. The laughter turned into a whoop of delight.

Vernon wondered what had happened.

"Oh, my!" she exclaimed. "My car!"

"What about it?"

George wanted me to meet him in Jarvis for dinner."

Vernon considered this. Jarvis was a larger town about twenty miles away from Fairville.

"You left it there?" he asked, smiling.

"No! I don't like to drive at night, so I caught a bus into Jarvis." She laughed again and pointed at Vernon. "I took the Greyhound bus and parked my car there. And the bus station is right across the street from your office!"

Vernon Simms leaned back, glowering at Thelma. "I suppose you'll want a ride to pick it up."

"Well, I believe it's on your way," she said, still laughing hysterically at his expense.

SUSPENSE/CRIME

AY, THERE'S THE RUB

Author's note: I wrote the original version of this story years ago for a college creative writing class. Upon reading it, my professor told me I should become a writer rather than a teacher. "You can make money at this," he said. I declined, thinking it was better to have a steady paycheck, meager as it would be. It was the first time anyone other than my mother—whose opinions were suspect due to my being her son—ever told me I was actually good at this. The original version of this was my first attempt at writing a suspense story.

Dean Roberts arrived in Detroit over seventy-two hours before the president's speech. On that first day, he used his ticket to an evening's symphony performance at the auditorium where the speech would take place so he could hide the .45 caliber pistol in the auditorium's restroom. He'd stolen the gun the week before from someone who worked in the building where he worked. He'd heard that this person kept a pistol in his desk drawer after being threatened by someone he'd fired two years ago.

Ten minutes into the concert he left for the bathroom, figuring that would be a good time to find it empty. It was. He quickly balanced himself on the toilet seat, lifted a ceiling tile, and placed the loaded gun on top of the neighboring tile. He had made sure he wiped the gun and bullets to eliminate prints in case the secret service or police found the gun before Saturday's speech. He spent the first two nights at a nice but affordable hotel in town, but he would have to relocate for financial reasons. For the final night before the killing, he checked into what could best be described as a flophouse.

As Dean entered the dank hotel room, his nose curled. The smell of cigarette smoke bathed the room in a permanent stench. The sheets and curtains were, along with the walls, were yellow from years of exposure to the smoke, the slight fragrance of detergent failing to mask the embedded odor. The narrow strips of once-decorative wallpaper along the edge of the ceiling had begun peeling away in flaps and curls as if trying to break free and escape.

Grabbing his shaving kit, Dean stepped into the bathroom, a tiny closet with a shower stall because there was not enough room for a tub. An orange stain from years of dripping water funneled into the sink's grimy drain. Setting the shaving kit on the narrow edge of the counter surrounding the sink, he lifted the lid on the toilet and saw that the rust stains had set up shop in the porcelain bowl as well. He didn't bother looking into the shower. After emptying his bladder and shaving, Dean stepped back into the small bedroom. His nose was already getting used to the odors left by countless other patrons.

He undressed and lay on the lumpy mattress. In a few minutes he would be asleep, where he knew the dream lurked, but he couldn't stay awake forever, though he spent more time awake each night than asleep. An hour later, he had been asleep for perhaps ten minutes when the nightmare returned to haunt him like Poe's raven.

Every detail was always the same, including the man in the plaid shirt sitting beside him. Impatience filled the large venue as the audience waited. From the rafters above the stage, a large banner declared, "United Auto Workers: We Keep America Driving." A podium with the seal of the President of the United States stood dead center near the front of the stage. Seven microphones stood guard on the podium, as if they could stop what was about to happen.

The Detroit chapter of the UAW, where the once-powerful union's headquarters were located, was there to see the man they had supported for president, only to feel betrayed when he suddenly pushed through legislation that angered the union. This action resulted in the man himself coming to Detroit to explain. The legislation called for additional safety features. The UAW believed the additions would drive the cost of cars up nearly ten percent, possibly cutting their worldwide market share, which had already been dwindling for years. This loss would likely result in layoffs.

The events unfolded in the dream the same way every time. Flanked by his security agents who took up strategic positions on the stage, the president stepped out to polite applause. He cracked a stale joke, drawing a comment from someone behind Dean, and started into his speech. The man Dean thought of as the assassin walked calmly from backstage, approaching from the president's left.

The secret service men noticed him but did nothing besides look puzzled at his entrance. One even nodded at the man. Their reactions said they knew him and didn't fear his motives or actions.

The assassin stepped to the president, who leaned over to listen to what he had to say, irritation at being interrupted dimming the smile. Then the knife came out. The man plunged it into the president's left side, piercing his heart as blood began spurting everywhere. Too late, the secret service agents rushed forward to grab the assassin, but the man did their job for them, jamming the knife into his carotid, a triumphant smile his final message. His blood pooled, mingling with the president's.

The dream returned three times during the night, each time rousing him for at least an hour before he was able to get back to sleep. Other dreams surely occurred, but this was the only one he could remember upon waking.

There was one difference in the final version of the dream, however, and that bothered him. No detail had ever been different before. The change wasn't big, but it was a change nevertheless. The dream had stopped suddenly and jumped back to the moment the assassin walked onto the stage. Then the same thing happened again: The assassin walked onto the stage, but before he stopped to speak to the president, the dream jumped back again as if Dean had hit a skip back button on a DVR recording of a program. Once awake, Dean didn't understand what it meant, and it worried him. It was like starting a car and hearing the engine make a troubling sound it never made before.

He'd first had the dream two months ago. At first, he saw it as just a nightmare and wondered where it had come from. It wasn't as if he hated the president. Hell, he wasn't even a member of UAW. His identical twin brother was, and he wondered if this was a dream triggered by an unrealized worry about Jay. He had called his brother to check on him, but he was doing fine. Besides, it was the president who was murdered in the dream, not Jay.

After three weeks of this nightly vision, the dream became more ominous. The president had managed in just one week to push a bill through Congress that mandated additional automobile safety features. After some pointed comments from the union, he announced a trip to speak to an audience of UAW members in Detroit about it. Plans and security had been hastily ironed out, and now the day for his speech had arrived.

These events led to a certainty that Dean was having a premonition, not a dream. The president would be assassinated unless someone did something to stop it. Because he was probably the only person in the world who could stop what would happen, he had reluctantly accepted the job given him by fate or God or whatever power of the universe it was that had caused the vision. He knew that timing would be crucial. Too early, and the mere fact the assassin had a knife, though suspicious, would not be enough to shoot him. Too late, and the president might be dead before the man could be stopped. Dean needed the knife to be in the assassin's hand. The fact that he was so familiar with the sequence of events helped, but he still worried.

Until that last version of the dream, the events were always the same. One man always commented on the joke, each time saying, "You did. You pushed that legislation." Another man sneezed just moments before the president strode onto the stage. The president was always dressed the same, complete with a blue tie with diagonal red stripes and a UAW pin, as if he had become a member overnight. Dean was always in the same place, third row near the center, just to the president's right.

Now, however, the change to the dream kept gnawing at him as he dressed. Dean wondered if the change meant anything. Did it mean the assassination would not happen? Was the assassin having second thoughts? He wasn't sure.

He would stop by Jay's house around noon for lunch and a quick visit, pretending to have just arrived in town. He had arranged to borrow Jay's event pass as well as his UAW badge, which showed a picture that looked just like Dean. The badge had to be shown with the ticket to gain entrance. Jay hadn't been interested in attending, and Dean had convinced his twin to let him go instead, telling Jay, "I just want to see a sitting president once in my life. A bucket list thing." He never told anyone about the dream, including Jay. He knew how crazy it all sounded.

Dean made it easily through the security detail when he arrived. He'd shown Jay's UAW badge and ticket before passing through an airport metal detector set up especially for the event. Then he veered toward the men's restroom, praying the gun would still be there. No news programs had reported a gun being found, but such news may not have been released to the public.

As he entered the restroom, two other men were there, one washing his hands, the other at a urinal. Dean stepped into the stall below the hidden gun and locked the door, praying the event's hasty preparations would prevent the gun from being found. He waited until the last man left. The event was starting in just a few minutes, and he needed to hurry. The assassination would happen less than a minute after the president finished the lame joke.

Once alone, Dean climbed onto the seat and lifted the ceiling tile, praying the weapon was there. His hand found only the top side of the neighboring tile. Nausea gripped him. *It wasn't there! It had been found by the security detail!* The sudden shock caused him to stumble a bit, causing his hand to move a few inches. Relief washed over him as his hand grazed the weapon.

Grabbing it, he quickly dropped from the toilet seat just as a man entered and strode up to a urinal. Dean flushed and stepped out of the stall, striding to the sink to wash his hands, aware of the gun pressing into his side beneath his coat. It felt like a coiled monster, aching to spring forth and take lives, serving the purpose for which it was created.

Dean washed quickly, left the bathroom, and nearly ran to the doors of the auditorium.

The first thing Dean noticed as he entered was the now familiar banner waving slightly in the breeze rushing from the air conditioning vents like an old friend greeting him. *Hi, Dean. Welcome back to your nightmare.*

Walking down the aisle to his left, he arrived at the third row and saw the empty spot beside the man in the plaid shirt that he'd never seen before— but had. The man's presence punctuated the unlikely reality of what was happening. He excused himself as he edged between knees and seatbacks, sitting down just in time to hear the sneeze and stand for the president.

As Dean stood up, he wasn't sure he could remain standing. His legs trembled from the rush of adrenalin and debilitating fear that flooded his veins. The reality that he was about to shoot a man in front of a thousand witnesses hit him, and he had to concentrate on not throwing up. Despite the chill he'd felt upon entering the auditorium, he was sweating now as if he had entered a sauna.

Dean recognized the president's clothing choice and his smile and wave as reality again aligned with the dream. The president stopped as he approached the podium and held both hands in the air and waved again. Dean felt as though he was watching a movie that he'd seen a hundred times already. *Déjà vu* didn't approach how odd he felt.

The president stepped to the podium, smiling as though every person in the room was solidly behind his car safety legislation. Dean began mentally checking off each move and nuance as they occurred.

"It's great to see so many smiling faces. I thought for a moment I'd taken a wrong turn or something," the president said, chuckling at his joke. Dean realized he was mouthing the words along with the president.

He heard the man's voice that he'd heard so often. "You did. You pushed that legislation."

Then Dean did something he hadn't done in any of the dreams. He turned around to look at the man who had commented on the joke. His gaze was met with a startled look. "Jay? You feelin' alright?"

Jay? The man thought he was Jay. The man knew Jay, of course. Dean nearly corrected the man but stopped himself just in time. Then he realized the man had asked him if he was feeling okay. He felt the room swimming. He must be pale, and his face was covered in sweat.

Nearly in a panic, Dean turned back to the stage. The assassin was already near the president. The moment was there. In seconds, the man would lean over. Speak to the president. Pull the knife. Shove it between ribs. Then take his own life.

Dean's body took over. Panicked, he pulled the gun and aimed it toward the assassin. He squeezed the trigger. The sound of the shot echoed through the room, deafening those close by. Screams and shouts burst from the crowd as Dean felt his arm being grabbed. Someone was wrenching him to the floor. Then several men were on him, their combined weight crushing him.

Amid the noise and mayhem, Dean struggled for breath and grunted, "He has a knife! He was going to kill the president! He was going to kill the president!"

His voice was drowned out by the chaos. He stared into the face of the man who knew Jay and had commented on the joke. He was one of the men who had wrestled him to the floor.

Dean screamed up at the man, "Is he safe?! Is the president safe?!"

The look the man returned was unexpected. He looked as though Dean had just asked if the moon was really made of cheese. "What are you talking about?" the man shouted above the din and chaos.

"The president! Is he alright?!"

The man's brow creased as if he didn't understand the words. Confusion washed over the man's face as the secret service arrived and turned Dean over, slamming him onto his stomach.

Dean managed to strain his neck to look at the stage as he was handcuffed, lifted, and hurried from the room. As he did, the meaning of the man's consternation became evident. The president lay in a pool of the bright, red blood that was blooming from the center of his chest. The assassin stood nearby, shock and disbelief, as well as the president's blood, covering his face. Then the assassin glanced around, touched the outside of his jacket pocket, and ducked backstage.

As Dean watched this and the secret service men hustled him away, he wondered about the role of fate in the universe. Was he meant to commit this murder? Did we have any free will at all? Were they all just puppets to destiny? He had only the questions, though. The answers would never come.

Three days later, Dean sat on his bed in an isolated jail cell. This cell was located down a short hallway that stretched from another locked door.

Jay had finally visited yesterday. Dean had tried to explain, but Jay wasn't interested in listening. He was suspended while the Secret Service and FBI investigated him, despite Dean's insistence he had nothing to do with any of this.

Dean had told the FBI and anyone who would listen about the dream. The man Dean had thought of as the assassin turned out to be one of the president's personal assistants. Nobody believed Dean, despite how he'd seen the man touch his breast pocket where the knife had been hidden. Obviously, the man had gone backstage and hidden the knife. More than once, Dean wondered if, like him, the man thought about fate and destiny.

Dean had asked to speak to the man, but his request had been denied. He couldn't really blame anyone. His story sounded insane, even to him, despite all the evidence to Dean that everything was just as he'd thought.

Dean knew that his mistake was firing too soon. Otherwise, the dream had happened in every detail he remembered up to the shooting, and once again he considered the change to the dream in its last version. Everyone thought he was lying. Because nobody caught the president's assistant with a knife, their conclusion was logical.

Dean had been told by his court-appointed attorney he wouldn't be put to death, but only because Michigan did not have the death penalty, having banned it in 1963. The lawyer suggested Dean plead guilty and expect to serve life in prison without parole, since that was the most the court could impose. The attorney refused to listen to the story of the dream, and Dean wondered if that spurring event wasn't at least grounds for an insanity plea. John Hinckley had managed it after shooting Ronald Reagan. Hinckley had eventually been released from the psychiatric hospital where he'd been held and treated for thirty-five years. One difference, of course, was that Reagan had survived. Dean knew he would never get out, even if they thought he was crazy and sentenced him to serve his time in a psychiatric hospital.

As he sat alone in his isolated cell, Dean looked up as he heard the locked door at the end of the hall open and close. Hard-soled boots echoed as someone approached. When his visitor arrived, Dean looked up into the face of Armstrong, one of his guards, a large man with blond hair and beefy arms that suited his name.

"Hey, Armstrong. How ya doin'?" Dean asked.

"Okay," Armstrong said, staring down at Dean.

"So, what's up? Do I have a visitor?"

"Nope. Just me."

Dean nodded and looked into Armstrong's eyes. They were angry eyes. Hate and rage poured from them, causing Armstrong's jaw to harden and set like concrete.

"Been waitin' to have some time alone with you," Armstrong said. Fear rippled through Dean, causing the hair on his neck to stand. "You killed the best president this country's ever had."

Dean looked at the floor and swallowed in an effort to generate some saliva. "I didn't mean to. I was actually—"

At the sound of the click, Dean looked up. He

was staring down the barrel of Armstrong's service revolver. The hole filled his sight, looking like a tunnel that led to eternity.

"You bastard!" Armstrong yelled.

The gunshot echoed off the walls of the hallway.

Armstrong dropped his weapon and raised his hands as the door at the end of the hallway burst open and other guards scurried through. Armstrong looked at Dean's dead body, which was slumped over onto the floor and bleeding from a large hole in his chest, and began to sob.

Frank Gillman was cleaning out his desk. The vice-president, or rather the new president, had his own personal staff, and Frank had never cared much for the vice-president anyway. He had nearly finished packing the last box when Victor Marquette, the late president's press secretary, walked in.

"So, you heard about the guy who shot Thompson?" Victor said, half-sitting on the edge of Frank's desk.

"You mean Roberts? What about him?" Frank had been too busy to even look at a TV. His nerves were pretty well shot, and mostly he wanted to go home and think about how near he'd come to dying that week.

"One of the jailers shot him stone-cold dead."

Frank looked at Victor as if he'd spoken Greek. "What?"

"Yeah. He shot him. Loved Thompson, apparently, and killed the guy who did it."

"Well, to my way of thinking, the guard saved the country and the state of Michigan lots of money. They should pin a medal on the guy," Frank said, lifting a box.

"Did you hear what the guy was saying?"

"What guy?"

"Roberts, dummy. If you can't keep up, take notes. He talked about you and some crazy dream he had."

Frank stared at Victor. The guy who shot Thompson mentioned him? "Really?" Frank wasn't sure he wanted to pursue this, but he knew someone would mention it to him eventually since the story would not stop with Victor, of that Frank was certain. He'd rather hear it from someone he knew and not one of the vultures from the press, though they'd probably get their turn.

"Yeah. Said he dreamed that you were going to kill Thompson at the speech. With a knife, no less. Said he was trying to save the president, not kill him."

"Where did you hear this?"

Victor squinted at him. "I'm the press secretary. I hear everything."

It was obvious Victor wouldn't reveal his source, though it would probably be easy to find out. Secrets in Washington lasted about four minutes. Meanwhile, Frank did his best to appear as nonchalant as possible under the circumstances. "Why would I do that?"

"Yeah, that's what I said. Anyway, the nutcase said he dreamed over and over you stepped out on the stage like you did and pulled a knife and stabbed

132

Thompson in the heart then killed yourself."

"Oh. Well, I didn't," Frank said and started to leave the office. He needed to sit down somewhere—anywhere, as long as it was private.

"What were you doing out there on the stage that day anyway?" Victor asked, though not as if he believed the nonsense. Frank stared at Victor for a moment. Victor had spent twenty-three years as a journalist, Frank thought. It was natural for him to ask questions. Frank did his best to relax, but his stomach was in knots.

"He'd asked me to come out and pretend to say something to him. He planned to say I'd told him he had to leave early to cut the questions short if they became difficult," he said. "He and I were the only ones who knew about it," he added in case Victor started asking the Secret Service guys questions.

"Oh," Victor said, "nice plan. Gonna miss the old guy."

"Yeah. Me too." Frank hurried away and out to his car, unlocking it with his key fob and tossing the box into the back. He'd have to go back for the rest, but right now he needed to think and quell the nausea that had taken up residence in his gut. He sat behind the wheel and contemplated life and death and how quickly one could switch to the other.

Taking out his cell, he looked at the wallpaper image of his daughter. The picture had been taken in March at her fourth birthday party. She had helium balloons rising from where they'd been tied in her hair, pulling strands up. Her grin showed the extent of her happiness. He thought of how she didn't know her life was in danger because of him.

Panicked tears burned his eyes.

His phone rang, startling him so badly he dropped it to the car's floorboard. Groping for the phone, he grasped it and glanced at the screen to see who was calling. It was as if staring at his daughter's picture had somehow conjured the caller at that precise moment. Knowing he couldn't avoid answering, despite desperately wanting to, he pressed the button to connect.

"You still owe me the money," a voice said. "Over two-hundred thousand and rising every day. Gambling debts don't just disappear, and I ain't some nightmare that will go away either, you know," the man said, unaware of the irony.

"Yeah, I know."

"Since—well—you didn't exactly have to follow through on the last small task, we could work out another favor. That way, that cute little girl of yours can stay alive and happy. You know, one hand washes the other?"

Frank had heard the man on the other end of the call use that expression before and dreaded what the man on the line might suggest and knowing he would have to do his bidding or his daughter would die a horrible, terrifying death. The man on the call had even once told him he knew a man with "certain proclivities." Frank had needed no elaboration, and each time he thought about the threat, he would break into a cold sweat.

His own life didn't matter, only his daughter's. He would happily sacrifice his own for her. His wife, Rebecca, would raise their daughter without him. She would grieve the loss of her husband, even hate him if what he had to do was so public as assassinating the President of the United States.

"What kind of favor?" Frank waited for the other shoe to drop, knowing full well it was dropping on top of him.

PRISONER OF THE MIND

Author's note: This story has some thriller elements that involve science gone mad. I hope you have as much fun reading it as I had writing it. But, goodness, sometimes these characters take me on quite a ride.

Andrea sat alone in the back seat of the car as it slid down the street, taking her somewhere she didn't know. The driver looked familiar, but she couldn't quite place him. Now that all she saw was the back of his head, she was unable to think about who he might be, only that she knew him from somewhere.

His voice had seemed familiar, too, but like his face, finding the memory was just out of reach. About the only memory that felt even remotely solid was that she'd been a teacher—or was still one. She wasn't sure anymore.

That morning, she had awoken to think she was late for work, not remembering she no longer needed to be there. She'd sat upright as fast as she could and swung her feet to the floor. The moment she'd managed to stand, the door to her bedroom had opened, and the man who was now her driver had stepped into the room.

"Get out!" she'd screamed. She was still in her nightgown, and this man had just waltzed in as if it were his room.

"It's okay," the man had said. "You're fine."

"I'm late for work! Who are you?"

"Just settle down. You don't teach anymore."

A woman she also thought she recognized had appeared and helped her get dressed after she shooed the man away. Andrea and the woman talked, but the woman refused to tell her who she was, no matter how many times Andrea asked.

Finally, Andrea demanded, "You keep changing the subject when I ask who you are. Why?"

To that the woman smiled as if placating a child. "Don't worry. Everything will be fine. You'll see."

The couple had escorted her to the car she now rode in, strapping the seatbelt around her after seating her in the backseat as though she might be incapable of doing it on her own. The woman had joined the man in the front. Andrea listened to their conversation, hoping for a clue as to who they were and where they were taking her. They talked as if they thought she couldn't hear.

"This can't go on," the man said. "You see that, right?"

"Yes."

"Who knew it would end up like this?"

"Greg. Greg knew."

He waved at the woman dismissively. "If you ask me, Greg doesn't know his ass from a hole in the ground."

"He knew this would happen."

"Based on what?"

"His research."

"I'd say it was a lucky guess."

"Lucky or not, now we have to deal with it."

Andrea listened, confused. They seemed to be dancing around a topic. And who was this Greg? Her head started to hurt, and she reached a hand up to rub where it felt tender. Was that a scar?

Why could she remember nothing? At that moment she wasn't even sure she'd been a teacher. A flash of an image suggested she might have worked in a laboratory somewhere. She remembered a room full of people in lab coats and small animals in cages. Microscopes and computers, along with the paraphernalia of science, were arranged on desks and tall counters.

She recalled sitting in a chair in this lab but unable to move, unable to stand or move her arms or legs. Immobile.

Fear began to grip her chest.

"Where are you taking me?" she asked the backs of the heads. When they didn't respond, she said, "I asked where you're taking me! I demand to know!"

Glancing at each other, the man turned his attention back to the road as the woman turned in her seat a bit to face her. "You're fine. We're taking you to visit someone."

"Who?"

The woman looked at the man then back at Andrea. "He's a doctor. A specialist."

"A specialist in what?" Andrea could tell her questions were upsetting the woman. Her agitation grew clearer with each one.

The woman cleared her throat. "The brain."

"What's wrong with my brain?" Andrea wanted to know, yet she didn't. Her lack of memory was certainly a part of the answer.

Instead of answering, the woman asked, "What did you have for breakfast yesterday morning?" Her eyes told Andrea the woman knew the answer would be "I don't know," so Andrea didn't answer. The woman turned back to face forward, leaving Andrea to wonder why she couldn't remember.

"Was I a math teacher?" she asked. This time the demanding tone was replaced with desperation.

"Yes," the woman said without turning her head.

"Then why was I strapped to a chair in a laboratory?"

This brought the woman's head back to face Andrea. After a slight pause, she replied, "You must have dreamed that." Andrea knew she hadn't, though. She might have believed she'd dreamed it had the woman not turned her head to her, but she could see the lie in the woman's eyes as well as hear it in her voice.

They pulled up to a razor-wire topped fence and gate where an armed guard let them through. Andrea noticed the coils of razor-wire were doubled, attached to metal arms that leaned both toward the inside of the compound and the outside. It was designed not only to keep people out, but also to keep others in. Foreboding swelled in her chest.

As they entered a stark, white building with a sign out front with the words "Bldg. 14" as the only identifier, they were stopped again. The man and woman produced credentials of some sort, and they were allowed into the barren hallways. Instead of pictures or other decoration to liven the atmosphere, these walls were bare. Moments later, she was seated in a small office, the man and woman flanking her as if they expected her to run.

A short, balding man in a lab coat and black horn rim glasses entered through a door behind the desk. "Don, Holly," he said, acknowledging the man and woman with a nod and an insincere smile. Sitting, the pudgy man looked at Andrea and with that same empty smile.

"Good morning, Ms. Campbell," he said. "How are you today?"

"We've met?" she said, though she had no memory of it.

"Of course, though I suspect you don't recall it. I'm Doctor Greg Highsmith."

Greg? She'd heard that name recently, though she couldn't remember where. "Why am I here?"

Dr. Highsmith continued smiling. "I will tell you, though by this afternoon you won't remember what I said."

Andrea sat forward a bit. She would do her best to prove him wrong.

"Five months ago, you volunteered for a program, an experiment concerning memory. The government is trying to find a way to make the human brain more like a computer. Now, it's been said the brain is like the world's most sophisticated computer, but that's not entirely true. That's because a computer has complete and total recall. Press a few buttons, and entire manuscripts of books hundreds, even thousands of pages long, pop onto the screen. Enter a few words into a search engine query frame, and hundreds of thousands of related links are clicks away in seconds.

"So, you see, the government wanted to find out if science could alter the brain in such a way as to create that same efficiency. We advertised for people willing to become subjects for our study, live with us for a year while the experiments were done, and you responded. As I recall, you mentioned teachers are so grossly underpaid—and I agree they are—that taking a year off for twice the money was a godsend.

"So what happened?"

"Well, one team of researchers felt an implant was the best method to increase the brain's efficiency. I didn't agree with the them. I felt chemicals were the answer. After all, the body is nothing more than an electro-chemical organism. Anyway, because they'd managed to build an implant before my team could develop an acceptable chemical, their idea was accepted. You, I'm afraid, are the result."

Afraid? Why afraid? "But I can't even remember what I had for breakfast."

"Exactly."

"So instead of giving me a super memory, this implant has robbed me of my memory entirely?"

Doctor Highsmith glanced at the man and woman before he spoke. "Well, not exactly."

"Then what, exactly?"

"The fact is the implant worked. Your memory became, well, amazing. You could glance at a page of manuscript and recite it verbatim. We opened copies of all of Shakespeare's plays online, and had you scroll through the pages as fast as the screen would move. In two minutes, you knew them all word-for-word."

"Then why can't I remember anything now?"

"Because, unfortunately, there were side-effects."

"What do you mean?"

"Within two weeks of receiving the implant, you were a raving lunatic, and as an unforeseen effect of the implant, extremely powerful, physically. We had to confine you to a padded room, even though we had you strapped to your bed. You'd get loose and smash yourself into the walls, so two feet of cotton padding protected you from harming yourself."

"So what happened? I'm not bouncing off the walls now."

"We removed the implant."

Andrea considered this for a moment. "Then why am I not back to the way I was before the implant? Why is my memory basically gone?"

"The implant was lodged in the hippocampus, the part of the brain that controls memory. When it was removed, there was damage to that part of the brain. It was unavoidable, I'm afraid."

"So I was brought here for you to tell me this so I can forget it by this afternoon?"

"No, you were brought here to see if we can reverse the damage."

"With what? Another experimental operation?"

Doctor Highsmith shrugged. "If it comes to

that, but first we're going to try chemicals."

"You said you hadn't developed them yet."

"No, what I said was my team hadn't developed an acceptable chemical. The people in charge of this experiment weren't satisfied that it would work or be safe. Now," he said, raising his hands palms up, signaling they weren't so concerned anymore.

"What if I say no?"

"You've already said yes when you signed the contract to be a subject."

"I'm not a subject. I'm a person."

"Ms. Campbell, without memories, you're just a shell."

"I remember being a teacher."

"There are some residual memories, and in fact, we've found that for a short time, you will remember everything clearly. But most of your long-term memory is gone. For instance, tell me the names of your children?"

Andrea stared at him blankly. "I have children?"

"You tell me. Do you?"

Andrea did her best to concentrate, trying in vain to conjure a memory of anything that would answer that question. Childbirth. First lost tooth. Hell, even changing a diaper. But nothing came to her. Finally, she asked. "Do I have children?"

Doctor Highsmith sighed. "No. In fact, we only chose subjects without any family ties."

"Why no family ties?" Andrea considered correcting him once again that she wasn't a subject, but she didn't want to hear again that without memories she was just a shell.

"We didn't want any...complications...in case something like this happened. Your husband died in a car accident three years ago, and you haven't spoken to his family since. You claim you didn't like them, and the feelings were mutual. You're an only child, and your parents died when you were in your twenties. Your father had a heart attack. Your mother died of cancer. You have no other relatives since your parents were only children as well, and all their parents are deceased."

This brought a new question to mind. "How old am I?"

"Thirty-seven."

"Do I have a teaching job?"

"For now because you took a sabbatical, but without the ability to remember anything, I'm afraid it would be useless to return—unless we can do something about your memory."

Andrea stared into the corner of the room while she considered what to do. She felt more like a prisoner than a research volunteer. Still, the doctor was right. She would have to do whatever she could to restore her ability to remember. Otherwise, he was right that she was just a shell.

"I want one thing," she said. "I want some paper and pens to write down facts about myself so I can read them every day to remember who I am. I don't want to wonder if I have children or not, or if I really was a teacher."

Doctor Highsmith offered his same painted-on smile. "Certainly. In fact, I believe I have some right here." Reaching into a drawer, he took out a legal pad and a few pens and handed them to Andrea. Then he turned to the man and woman and said, "Take Ms. Campbell to her room. We've reserved 412 for her."

"You go ahead," the man said to the woman. "I've got to talk to Doctor Highsmith for a moment." The woman left with Andrea.

"Are you sure that's wise?" Don asked when the women were gone.

"Am I sure what's wise?" Dr. Highsmith said.

"Giving her paper and pens. Suppose she writes a letter to someone in the press or something?"

"And say what? 'I'm being held captive because I can't remember anything?' Don't be ridiculous. By this afternoon she won't remember anything we said in here. Hell, she won't remember you, me, or Holly."

"So what's the plan?"

"We'll give her the drugs and see what happens. If they work, great. If not, well, the agency has a plan in place for that."

"What kind of plan?"

"Above your pay grade, I'm afraid." His meaning was clear. Andrea Campbell would be killed regardless of the outcome. If she remembered, she'd be a liability. If she didn't, she would be an unnecessary cost, another failed subject in their tests. They just wanted to find out if the drugs would work. Success or failure would both result in the need to kill the guinea pig, just as it often happened in other labs and with other tests.

On the way to her room, Andrea kept repeating

in her mind the details of the conversation that pertained to her. She was determined to remember who she was and what had happened to her. She would write those details down, read them every day. Perhaps then she might begin to remember over time.

When they arrived at room 412, Holly made sure Andrea was comfortably sitting and writing on the pad before leaving to meet Don at the exit. They walked to their car in silence, each regretting ever getting involved with this study. Holly imagined everyone who knew something about this research was being watched.

As if prompted by Holly's thoughts, Doctor Highsmith looked down from his window as Don and Holly left the building together. They had become a liability, which saddened him, but the situation was what it was. He watched them climb into the car, unaware of the explosive device nestled beneath the chassis. As they exited the gate, the armed guard pressed a button activating the timer. It would take them at least forty minutes to drive to where they were going. The timer was set to go off in thirty. Dr. Highsmith counted any unintended casualties as victims of circumstance and nothing more.

Seven months later, Andrea sat in her room, reading her notes, or pretending to. In reality she no longer needed them. Apparently, the drugs Doctor Highsmith's team had created worked just as he'd hoped. Her memory was now more than simply intact. It was, as the good doctor had put it in the interview when she'd received the pad of paper and pens, amazing.

She had hidden these effects from the scientists who spoke with her daily. She didn't want them to know their concoction was a success. She would pretend to remember nothing, or next to nothing. Her sudden clarity of mind allowed her to always remember not to remember. She would make a show of reading their name badges to refer to them by name. She would always fail their memory tests. She was scamming them, and by the defeated looks on their faces, she was successful at it.

Of course, she knew this would inevitably lead to her being killed, her body disposed of in a way that guaranteed it would never be found. She felt sure they had enough highly corrosive acid on hand for that. She would just have to escape somehow.

Her mental powers gave her an edge. Doubly so, given that they had no idea her mind was sharp once again. Extremely sharp.

She had requested to be allowed to take walks in the compound outside her building. Because they thought her incapable of planning an escape, they were happy to oblige.

She had noticed the UPS delivery truck arrived like clockwork every Thursday afternoon around three. She'd been told this was a private corporate compound that performed tests for the government, so receiving UPS deliveries of such things as office and housekeeping supplies would be expected. It was the punctuality of the driver that led her to her escape plan.

She had noted that the conspicuous cameras

aimed at the doors and gates did not concern themselves with the compound itself, which would provide her all the cover she needed.

She had begun taking her walks from 2:45 until 3:30 each day. On the day she chose to leave, she tore one edge from her bed sheets and stuck the strip into her blouse, which hung loosely on her to allow for room to hide the linen. She left her room and sauntered outside, taking her journey, as she usually did, over to the loading dock beneath her window four floors up. She noticed the UPS truck approaching the loading area and timed her arrival as the driver, with the help of the two loading dock employees, walked into the storage area, where boxes would be counted and paperwork signed.

Ducking under the vehicle on a side away from any cameras, Andrea pulled the strip of linen from beneath her blouse and tied her torso to the undercarriage of the large van. She cinched it tightly enough to lift her from the ground, using knots she had learned as a child to secure herself. The UPS van's chassis was high enough off the ground to still allow her nearly a foot of clearance between her back and the road beneath. She had been working out in her room, developing muscle tone she kept hidden beneath the baggy blouses she always wore.

Soon, the driver returned to his vehicle and drove through the gate before journeying into Washington with his hidden cargo.

By the time Andrea's disappearance was discovered, she was sitting in a room with several news editors with the Washington Post, dirty and tired, but alive. The editors' jaws hung slack at the story she told, which she verified by asking to see any book in the building, chosen at random. She flipped through the first ten pages, glancing at each page for less than a second, handed the book to one of the editors, and began to recite what was on the pages without missing one word.

IF AT FIRST

Author's note: I wrote this story with the idea that it would go in one direction only to have the characters take the story somewhere I never thought it would go. My original idea for an ending was even darker than the one here. I won't tell what that ending is since this story veered very early, and the other story is still percolating, waiting to be written.

Sarah felt a wave of nausea and dizziness hit her and braced her hand against the wall as she waited for one of her building's two elevators to finally arrive. *Damn things take longer every day,* she thought. She'd skipped breakfast because she was running late, and the job interview was too important to reschedule. Besides, rescheduling would just equal *never mind.* Her low blood sugar, anxiety, and the feeling of being rushed had mingled to cause the brief spell.

Once it passed, she took her compact from her purse and gazed into the tiny mirror to check her makeup and hair. Noticing a dot of stray lipstick, Sarah wiped at a corner of her mouth with her index finger. Her raven hair was still in place; the rest of her makeup remained unblemished. She looked down at her attire—a navy blue pencil skirt with matching blazer and a white short-sleeve blouse—and adjusted the ruffle lining the blouse's placket.

The elevator finally arrived with a *ding* and she boarded it, thankful to be alone, but the relief was temporary. She heard rushing footsteps and a hand darted between the nearly closed doors, which bounced open again. A tall man about her own age with shaggy, brown hair stepped on and offered an apologetic smile.

"Sorry," he said, "running late."

Proffering a polite smile, she tried to hide her disappointment of having to ride the dozen floors to street level with him. She noticed that besides needing a haircut, the guy could use a shave to remove the day-old growth. His beige chinos and a red polo shirt both looked as if they came out of the Goodwill bargain bin. She hoped again she would get the job she was interviewing for so she and Ed could move to a better area of New York. Midtown Tenth Avenue wasn't bad, exactly, but not good either. She wanted to live closer to the park. If she wanted to get there now, she had to take a crosstown bus or walk, which if the traffic sucked, was faster. She dreamed, like many other New Yorkers, of living on the Upper East Side in the seventies or eighties, or maybe even on Fifth Avenue with a view of the park.

As the elevator began its sluggish descent, the guy said, "I'm Paul," and stuck out his hand to shake hers.

Sarah looked at his hand and noticed he needed a manicure before sending an I-don't-really-want-to-talk-to-you-but-I-will-if-you-insist smile in his direction. Reaching out, she reluctantly took his hand and shook it. His grip was firm without going overboard and she matched his pressure. "I'm Sarah," she said out of necessity but said nothing more.

His smile was making her nervous. She could almost feel him undressing her with his eyes. The elevator seemed even slower than usual as it crept past the tenth floor. She began to hope someone else would join them, preferably another woman, but she'd settle for one of the middle-aged salesmen who lived in the building.

"So, you live in the building?" he asked.

"Yes," she said.

"Me too," he said. "Moved in last week. Guess we haven't run into each other 'til today."

Sarah did her best to ignore him, but he wasn't getting the hint.

"I notice you're not wearing a wedding ring or anything. Single? Or too liberated to follow convention?"

Okay, now he was moving from annoying to creepy. "I'm one-hundred-percent lesbian," she lied, hoping it would make him stop coming on to her.

"Then who was that athletic dude who left your place around ten-thirty last night?"

Her mouth dropped open and her heart shifted into high gear. She stared at him, blinking as the heat of her blood rushed to her cheeks. He'd been watching her?

"How did you know that? Are you stalking me?" Her voice was scared and angry all at once.

"No," he said as if to reassure her. "I just, you know, saw him leaving. It just got me to wondering."

"How do you know which apartment's mine?" *And why would you ask if I live in the building if you already knew?* she wondered.

He shrugged. "Just observant, I guess."

She looked up at the floor numbers over the doors. Passing seven. *Why the hell was it so slow?*

"You didn't answer my question," he said.

She looked at him, her brow furrowed in irritation. "What question?"

"If you're a lesbian, who was the guy leaving your place last night?"

Her anger at being interrogated, besides the stupidity of his assumption that lesbians couldn't have male friends, prevented her from saying what she wanted to. She was afraid she might start hitting him if she lost her temper. She wanted to tell him that, yes, she was straight if it was actually any of his fucking business, and that the muscular guy was her fiancé, who was leaving for work because he worked the graveyard shift and was saving up for the engagement ring. She wanted to warn this jerk that if he said one more personal thing to her, she was going to tell the cops he tried to rape her. She even considered ripping her new blouse to make it seem true if it came to that. Hell, he'd practically raped her with his eyes a few times already anyway. Instead of telling the truth, though, she told another lie. "He's my brother. His favorite pastime is stomping the shit out of guys who bother me. And right now, you're bothering me."

Rather than watch the twerp's reaction, she squeezed her eyes shut, hoping the damn elevator would speed up. They were definitely moving out soon. A lot of the men in her building could be disturbing, but this guy had created a whole new level of creepy. He was downright scary. She was used to guys undressing her with their eyes, but at least their mouths stayed shut.

She felt a jolt and opened her eyes. Shock washed over her as she realized the elevator had stopped, but not at the bottom floor. It had simply stopped.

"No, no, no, no, NO!" she screamed. "This isn't happening!"

She looked at Paul, who shrugged as if he had no place to be, which made her wonder about him. Hadn't he said he was running late? He opened the little door to the phone and pulled it out. The broken cord dangled from the receiver. "I guess we're stuck here for a while," he said, holding up the useless phone.

Her glance jumped around the elevator car, seeking an exit.

"There's no way out," Paul said. "At least not that you'd be able to use in that dress."

"What do you mean?"

"There's a trap door in the ceiling," he said, pointing, "but you'll ruin your clothes if you try it. Grease and dirt are everywhere up there. Not to mention that's where the rats live."

Sarah stared at the hatch as if rats might pour through at any moment. It was the worst thing about New York. She loved everything else about the city, well except for creeps like Paul, but the rats were the worst. Sometimes when she and Ed were coming home from a night out, they would see them scurrying about in the gutters. If rats were up there, she would rather wait until someone rescued them, even if it meant staying with this creep.

Smiling at Sarah, Paul slid down to the floor to wait. "Might as well relax. It could be hours before they notice we're trapped here." She considered screaming but decided to wait a bit for that.

She looked at the floor and then at her nice clothes. "No way am I sitting on these disgusting floors."

Paul shrugged. "Have it your way. You might at least want to take off those heels."

She looked at her shoes as if she'd forgotten she was wearing any. Figuring she shouldn't worry about getting the bottoms of her feet dirty, she slipped off the stilettos.

Paul reached for one, but she stopped him. "Hey! Just keep your hands off my shoes, okay? What are you, some kinda perv? Got a thing for women's shoes?"

He managed to look offended. "No. I was just going to hand them up to you."

"Leave them there. I'll be slipping them on the second this deathtrap starts up again."

He chuckled, irritating her. She squinted down at him and said, "What's so funny?"

"Everyone always thinks an elevator's a deathtrap. Like we're gonna run outa air."

She ignored him. She didn't like his sense of humor, if it could be called that. Sense of irritation was more like it. As she stood there, hating him, she was reminded that the guy seemed to know a lot about her, like where her apartment was and when Ed had left for work last night. He said he'd just noticed is all, but even as he had said, Ed had left around ten-thirty. What would this creep be doing out in the hallway at that time? Sure, it could be innocent, like he was taking his trash to the garbage chute, but the more she considered it, the more she wanted an answer.

She decided to keep an eye on him without seeming to. She glanced around the inside of the elevator, but she was noticing him and what he did by keeping him in her peripheral vision. Occasionally, she would glance directly at him when she was certain he wasn't looking up at her. One of these times, she noticed him looking at her legs as if she had worn a skirt for him to admire her legs while sitting on the floor of an elevator.

Becoming uncomfortable being near him, she stepped toward the opposite corner. He pretended to ignore her. Finally, the need to know what he'd been doing in the hallway at ten-thirty last night overwhelmed her.

"I gotta ask," she said. "What were you doing out in the hallway at ten-thirty at night that you saw Ed leaving?"

Paul looked up at her. His smile changed a bit.

"I'll be completely honest. I've been watching you, Sarah. You're a very attractive girl. Extremely, in fact."

"You shit!" she said. "You have been stalking me!"

"Not stalking," he said, keeping his voice maddeningly calm. "Just—well—watching." As he spoke, his gaze moved from her face down her body to her feet and back again, lingering on the more intimate areas.

"You're a real asshole, you know that?"

156

"Then who you get so sexy for? If you don't want some guy to fuck you, what're you doing dressing like that?"

"Like what?! This is business attire! Besides, just because I look sexy to men doesn't mean I want any of them to do whatever they want with me!"

"Sorry. I forgot. You're a lesbian," he said and turned his head toward the door. He let out a derisive laugh, "Pff-ha. Yeah, right."

"Listen, asshole! Even if I went naked in the hallways, it doesn't give you or anyone else the right to touch me. It's my body, and I give it to the people I want to give it to! And that definitely does not include you!"

Paul stood slowly as if exhausted. He took a deep breath, inhaling through his nose then exhaling through parted lips. "What makes you think I care whether you give it to me or I take it?"

Terror swept through Sarah as she realized she'd forgotten her situation. The creep had seemed mostly harmless before, no match to a knee in the groin, or too mild of a guy to do anything to her. For the first time, she realized what she was dealing with and froze.

Paul's hands moved fast as he grabbed her right wrist and squeezed with surprising strength. The force of the pressure made her cry out, and suddenly he was against her, pressing her body into the wall, his nostrils flaring as he breathed down into her face.

Sarah thought about defending herself with her knee, but her legs were like jelly. Even if she'd managed to raise her knee to kick him in the groin,

157

no force would be behind the blow. Her feeling of helplessness overwhelmed her, and she began to cry.

"Please," she whispered. "Please don't hurt me."

One hand was on her throat now, beginning to squeeze as he began popping the buttons from her top, one-by-one. She heard them clatter and bounce off the close walls and floor of the elevator as he pinched them off with a small tug.

"Please," she begged through the tightness of his grip on her throat. "Someone will come to get us out in a moment. Someone will catch you raping me. Please."

He looked at her with contempt. "You dumb bitch! I have a key to the elevator. I'm the one who stopped it. Nobody will think a thing because the other elevator still works."

With sudden clarity, Sarah knew she would not live through this. If she lived, he would go to jail, and he knew it. The thought that the inside of this elevator would be the last thing she ever saw made her weaker.

She looked at him despite her fears. He was holding up the brass key that operated the elevator. She had no idea how or where he got it. Her eyes shot to the panel and noticed where the key would go. As if everything had slowed down, she could see the jagged key slot aimed at "STOP." He was taunting her with the key, knowing she would see it as her lifeline and understanding that this lifeline was completely out of reach. He tossed the key over his shoulder, and she heard it clink and rattle in the far corner.

Then grabbing her top, he yanked viciously, sending the remaining buttons flying. He pulled at the bra, lifting it away from her body and exposing her breasts. Then he reached around her back, and seconds later the bra fell to the floor like a dead bird. Keeping one hand on her throat, he reached down with his other and tugged on the waist of the skirt, deftly undoing the hook and lowering the zipper with only one hand.

He wrestled her to the floor. As he finished pulling the skirt's zipper, he lay across her, one hand still on her throat, squeezing hard enough to prevent her from screaming but not hard enough to cause a loss of consciousness.

"No, no," she squawked as her hands flailed at his back, the air, the floor. Suddenly, one hand landed on one of her shoes. They were stiletto heels, the tips sharp and narrow with metal tips to prevent wear. She saw immediately what she had to do and spit into his face.

He pulled back in surprise, and she rammed the heel of the shoe into his left eye.

"Aaagghh!" he screamed as blood and fluid spurt from his eye, the heel of the shoe imbedded in the soft tissue like a nail in putty. He let go of Sarah and both hands went immediately to the wound, the soul of the shoe resting against his cheek. He rolled over in agony.

When she was free of his weight, Sarah rolled in the other direction, grasping for the golden key in the corner. Her hand fell upon it, and she scrambled toward the panel and the key slot. She listened to his agonized screams while she fumbled with the key. She kept trying to jam it home, but the key was refusing to cooperate. Just as she was about to give up, thinking he had fooled her into thinking this was the key, she saw her mistake. The key was upside down, making it impossible to slide the key in. As she flipped the key over, she dropped it to the floor again. She reached down, grabbed it. Standing, she rammed the key into its slot and turned it to the "ON" position. She felt the elevator car jump.

Immediately, Paul was on her again, grabbing her from behind. As he tugged her away from the panel, she managed to slide one hand down the buttons, signaling a stop at several floors. Sarah fought her attacker, praying someone would help her, hoping a hallway would be occupied as the elevator doors opened to reveal the attack. Without his hands around her throat, she had been screaming as loudly as she could.

Suddenly, hands were on her, pulling her away from Paul, wrapping around her upper arms and preventing her from fighting. She had the disoriented belief that someone had arrived to help Paul. That one would hold her while the other raped her, and the two would take turns.

"NO!" she screamed. "NO!" She struggled to get away from the person holding her. Then through the barrier of fear and panic, she heard a voice.

"Shhh. Shhh. It's okay now. Shhh."

Sarah looked around, her face a grimace of utter terror. A man who looked to be in his forties was holding her, shushing her. His eyes looked frightened, but caring, filled with sorrow. Two other

160

men were lifting Paul roughly to his feet, looks of disgust covering their faces as they saw the shoe sticking out of Paul's eye and the resulting blood.

Paul's zipper was open from where he'd tried to rape her, his shrinking penis now dangling there, and she was standing in the hallway with nothing but shreds of hose and her panties around her knees. Other than that, she was naked. She saw her bra lying on the elevator floor. The rest of her clothes were strewn about inside the elevator like more dead animals.

She suddenly realized she was exposed to some of her male neighbors and did her best to cover herself. One of the men, a tall man with a mustache, removed his sports coat and draped it over Sarah's shoulders. It was long enough to come to mid-thigh.

She looked at the man through her tears of rage and shame. "Thank you," she said, her voice hoarse. He just smiled awkwardly in reply, doing his best to pretend he'd seen nothing.

Soon, the police and an ambulance arrived. The medics saw to her first, leaving Paul moaning in pain on the hallway floor. They helped cover her better with a thin blanket and took her vitals. A female detective squatted nearby and spoke to her, asking how it happened. As she related the events, they sounded to her as though they'd happened to someone else or as if it had been a nightmare she was recounting to a friend. She looked around at the neighbors who had helped her. One was shirtless and wore shaving cream over half his face, the rest having been shaved away. She later found out he'd heard her screams and come running.

As the medics began working on Paul, another ambulance arrived. She lay back on the gurney and allowed herself to cry. The fear and pressure eased with each passing moment as she realized she would live. The detective had stuffed her torn clothing into a bag and sealed it. Evidence, she thought. She didn't care. She never wanted to wear any of it again.

When Ed arrived at the emergency room almost an hour later, he sat on the bed beside her and held her, rocking her back and forth like a mother rocking a baby, listening to her try to purge the memory with her tears. As Ed held her, Sarah realized how close she had come to dying in that elevator car. The curtain was drawn around her bed to allow for something resembling privacy, and she pretended to be alone with Ed in their apartment. The only real wounds were to her psyche. One part of her wanted to go home; another wanted never to enter that building again.

Soon, Ed told Sarah she should lie back and get some rest. "I need to go to the bathroom and get something to drink, coffee or a soda. I'll be back soon. You want anything?"

She shook her head, and Ed left the curtained cubicle, easing away to another area of the hospital's emergency department. He found the room he was looking for when he saw the uniformed policeman standing guard at the door. Ed approached him.

"You can't go in there," the officer said.

"I know. My fiancée was the victim. I just want to get a look at him," Ed answered.

162

The officer peered up and down the corridor before turning to Ed. "You make a move to open that door, and you'll be on the floor in two seconds."

"No problem. I just want to look at him. I swear," Ed answered. The officer nodded.

Ed stood in the doorway to the secure room, looking through a small circle of glass in the door until the attacker noticed him with his one good eye. He was heavily bandaged. The men stared at each other. The cop at the door was mostly ignoring Ed, and the doctor and nurse in the room with the man were otherwise occupied, so Ed shrugged his shoulders at him and frowned in an "oh well" gesture. Nobody saw Paul nod back at Ed.

Paul was not a novice at rape or murder, but he was new to being caught. After making sure nobody was watching, he looked at Ed and held up one hand, rubbing his fingers and thumb together in a "money" gesture. He'd be out soon on bail and would expect payment, even if he hadn't been successful. Payment, whether or not he'd been successful, was part of the deal, and Ed knew it.

Ed nodded almost imperceptibly. He would owe Paul something for his pain and trouble even though Sarah was still alive, and the quarter-million-dollar life insurance policy he'd taken out on her as they prepared to be married would not be paying. Yet.

After all, Ed thought, *if at first you don't succeed...*

HORROR

THE ABYSS

"If you gaze long into an abyss, the abyss will also gaze into you." – Friedrich Nietzsche

Author's note: This story was my second effort at writing a horror story. It came about when a friend said he wanted to put together a book of horror stories to release before Halloween one year. The book never materialized, but this story grew from that. I've always been a fan of horror fiction and early horror films. I would read anything with horror that someone told me was good, and early Stephen King novels became like cherished treasures. I always felt that children should be involved in such stories to make them truly scary. They are symbolic of innocence facing pure evil. I think that's what happens here. A few loose ends are left dangling to allow the reader to fill in those blanks, but that doesn't mean the story is incomplete. I may one day turn this story into a novel, but we'll have to see about that. A final note: Aka Manah is not a creation of my imagination. He is known in some religions as a demon.

Todd Landers lay in his bed listening to the tapping at his bedroom window, a tapping he'd not heard since his parents bought this house a month ago. He didn't know what time it was, but it was still dark outside nearly an hour after the insistent sounds woke him.

Todd didn't like the dark. His dad said there was nothing in the dark that wasn't there in the light, but Todd wasn't so sure. He had turned eleven a month ago and knew he was getting too old to be afraid of the dark, but although he knew that, he still could sometimes feel the hair on his neck stand up when he couldn't see well in darkness as black as his hair. He would imagine things. The darkness held disembodied hands reaching to grab him. It hid from view the things that were afraid of the light. Like the thing tapping at his window.

Tap-tap . . . tap. Rhythmic without perfect rhythm. Persistent but patient.

He shut his eyes, scrunching his face with the effort.

You're being stupid! his growing-up voice said. The voice that had begun expressing itself more often recently. The voice that told him monsters weren't real. The voice he still didn't believe.

Get up and go see. You'll feel better. You'll find it's nothing.

Gathering his courage, he flung his covers off and sprang from his bed. He stumbled to the window and yanked the curtain aside. Todd stared into the darkness, certain that a face more terrible than any Halloween mask would materialize in the darkness to hover in the air fifteen feet from the ground. It would grin at him with the knowledge of his fear, laughing as Todd's urine spilled to the carpet beneath his bare feet. Instead there was nothing, and certainly no urine, thank goodness.

Tap-tap . . . tap. The same rhythmic cadence. Todd squinted into the night and exhaled. He'd been holding his breath without realizing it. The tree. Just the damn birch tree. The dead one. Wind blew and the bare tree once more tapped his window. *Tap . . . tap-tap . . . scratch.* Nothing more than that.

Feeling sheepish, he returned to bed, determined to go back to sleep. He would talk to his dad tomorrow. His dad had mentioned cutting the dead tree down. Now, Todd would insist on it.

He lay there for a long time, listening to the wind and the tree and the tapping and scratching, as if the tree wanted in. Finally, he drifted into a restless sleep where ghouls chased him and no help came to answer his cries, where creatures, unseen even in daylight, licked at his calves and arms as if they thought he would be delicious.

The next morning, Todd's first thought was of the tree. Rising from bed, he went to find his father that sunny Saturday. He found him at the breakfast table drinking coffee and reading the newspaper.

"Dad, you know how you mentioned you wanted to cut down the dead birch tree?"

His father nodded, barely acknowledging him. "Mm-hmm."

"Well, I think we should do that today. It kept tapping against my window last night."

Greg put aside the paper and smiled at his son. "Did it scare you?"

"No. It was just tapping and keeping me awake."

"Okay, sport. We can do that first thing. You gonna help me?"

"Sure!"

They got the extension ladder and chain saw from the garage, and soon the tree was nothing more than ten-foot sections of trunk and branch. Then his dad cut these into firewood and kindling before they stacked it.

After the tree had become small pieces stacked beside the house, Todd stood looking at it. "You won't be tapping at my window again, will you?" he asked. A gust of wind swirled by, causing dead leaves to scatter with a sound resembling a librarian shushing talkative children.

As Todd and his father were cutting the tree down, Lilith, Todd's younger sister, stood in her bedroom, trying to figure out what she'd found in the woods behind their house.

Her newest treasure resembled a very large game board, but she didn't recognize this one at all, and the board was cold. Holding it was like holding ice cubes, despite the warmth outside. Lined markings resembling the runes she'd seen in a book once were painted on the board, which felt more like hard wax than paper or cardboard. Perfectly aligned along the board's four edges, full-size illustrations of standard playing cards stared back at her. The face cards looked angry, if not evil, and the number cards included likenesses that resembled the demons she'd once seen in a painting. All the drawings were in sequence from ace to king, with each edge donated to a suit. She stared at the board and felt her scalp tingle.

Lilith ran to the family room for the deck of playing cards. Hurrying back, she began placing the cards on their corresponding images.

She had placed a half-dozen cards when something or someone yanked the cards from her hand, scattering them in the air. She gave a surprised yelp and watched in awe as the cards landed neatly onto the board, aligned perfectly along the edges, though no longer in sequence. Now all four suits were represented along each border. She lifted the ten of diamonds along the edge where she knew the hearts should be and gasped, her mouth an oval, her eyes wide. Beneath the card the disturbing image of the board's ten of diamonds stared back as if drawings moving from one spot to another on a game board happened every day.

Not only that, but the cards now looked like the pictures, complete with demons and evil faces. She reached out to the ten of diamonds again and carefully picked it up from the board and stared at it. She dropped it as if stung when it reverted to its original image. The card fell into her lap before seeming to be snatched up by a breeze to take its place with the other cards on the board. The demon reappeared on the card.

Terror finally took hold. She was about to scream when suddenly the runes began crawling toward the board's center, shocking her into silence. Her throat was so tight, she wasn't sure she could have screamed anyway. The runes gathered together, and a pale, green smoke rose from them as if a small campfire had been built with the runes for fuel. She held her breath and stared as the smoke formed words in the air above the board.

Hello, Lilith.

Again, she gasped. "How do you know my name?"

The words disappeared as the smoke shifted and reformed. *I know many things.*

"You do?"

Yes.

"How old am I?" she asked to test whatever this was.

9.

"What's my favorite doll?"

You call her Belinda. Shift. *She's on your bed.*

The smoke remained in the air, hovering above the board, shifting and forming the words. Lilith wasn't sure what to do—both answers were right.

She forgot she was talking to smoke. She imagined she was talking to someone or something from another place, like some place far away. Another galaxy maybe. Maybe some civilization had learned how to communicate through these boards, and she'd been the lucky one to find this one.

"What's your name?" she asked.

Aka Manah. The smoke formed the words in the air.

"How do I pronounce that?"

Just call me Abyss," the smoke wrote.

"Abyss?" She said, pronouncing it like *abbess*. "That's a funny name."

The smoke shuddered as if in pain and melted into the air. New tendrils rose from the board. *You said it wrong.* Shift. *It's pronounced like amiss.*

"Oh. Sorry. Abyss," she said, pronouncing it correctly. "What else do you know?"

I know you are jealous of your brother. The smoke moved, reforming. *He gets all of your father's time.* More movement. *This also makes you angry with your father.* Shifting once again. *If you had him to yourself*—shift—*your life would be different.* Shift. *You would be fulfilled.*

Lilith had no idea how this thing knew her secret thoughts, not to mention the fact that smoke was writing by itself in the air. It was eerie. "How do you *know* all these things?"

Because I have always been here.

Her brow furrowed in confusion. "You've been here since we moved in?"

Since long ago before deserts ruled the earth.

This made things no clearer to Lilith. What was that supposed to mean? Rather than pursue this, she asked, "Why are you here?"

To play tricks on people.

"What kind of tricks?" She was getting used to talking to the smoke. She was already considering it as more like another person.

Fun ones. Would you like to play?

"Yes." She smiled.

Sneak into your brother's bedroom.

He's busy and won't come in.

Put his pillow under the bed.

"What's fun about that?"

He will wonder who moved it.

And why.

Lilith pictured Todd going to bed and

wondering where his pillow was. She imagined him searching and searching until he discovered it under the bed. Yes, that would be funny.

She said, "I'll be right back." Rising from where she'd been sitting on the floor, she walked to Todd's bedroom. She crept in and put his pillow under his bed, pushing it well beneath to hide it. Grinning to herself, she pictured him searching everywhere for it.

As she left the room, she giggled softly, closing the door behind her. She felt—tingly, in a way she'd never experienced before.

She returned to her room and the game board. "That was fun," she said, plopping down.

The board was lying there, silent and cold, but the cards were now back in their box, and the runes were back in place. She wondered about this and took the cards back out. The disturbing card images on the board were once again sequential and separated by suit. Frowning, she started laying the cards out again, expecting Abyss to take them from her and arrange them again. This time, however, she finished with nothing happening.

She glared at the cards lining the edges of the board, waiting for them to reshuffle themselves and for the green smoke to return, but nothing happened.

Disappointment took hold and she went outside, still thinking about what awaited her stupid brother at bedtime.

When Todd had come to bed, he noticed immediately his pillow had disappeared. He'd searched for five minutes until he found it beneath his bed, wondering how it got there and hoping Lilith had done it. It had bothered him, but now all thoughts of his pillow, along with any hope he might get a good night's sleep, were long gone.

The tapping had started again.

At first, he'd thought it was his imagination. Then he wondered if he was hallucinating. Finally, he decided it didn't matter because the tapping, real or imagined, meant he would not sleep tonight.

Tap-tap . . . tap . . . scratch . . . tap. On it went. Last night the sound had been frightening. Now, it was more than that. It was malevolent. Evil. The sound was a thousand devils come to take him away for an eternity of horrors too frightening for even his imagination to conjure. Worse, there wasn't a thing anyone could do about it.

He thought about going to the window and attempting to prove to himself that what was happening wasn't happening at all, but this time his fear wouldn't let him. Unlike last night, he knew this could never be anything as easily explained as the dead tree had been, so he lay there suffering the anguish of hopelessness as the moonlight cast strange shadows on his walls.

As he fretted, he glanced toward the window. The curtains were still pulled open from the night before. Or had he closed them and they had opened themselves? He couldn't remember. Did he see eyes staring at him from outside? No, it couldn't be. His window was almost fifteen feet above the ground.

Realizing he would never be able to sleep in this room, perhaps ever again, he leapt from his bed and bolted out the door into the hallway beyond. His heart hammering and the hair on his neck standing, he managed to hurry to his sister's bedroom door without something horrible grabbing his ankle and tumbling him to the floor to be whisked away into a void forever.

He quietly entered her room and stood there, listening to her soft breathing. She was asleep, and he needed a place to at least attempt to do the same. He crept to her bedside and lay silently on the floor, taking one of Lilith's teddy bears for a pillow. He had no covers, and a chill seeped from Lilith's closet, but he did his best to ignore it. Anything, even a freezer, would be better than his own bedroom right now.

Turning onto his side, he clenched his eyes closed. Nearly two hours later, he fell asleep, shivering, and replayed his horrors in his dreams.

The next morning as Lilith looked down on her brother, watching him sleep, she wondered if the missing pillow may have backfired on her. Had he been so frightened he came to sleep in her room? Had he figured out she had done it and decided to sleep in her room for revenge? She wasn't sure, but she knew she didn't like finding him there. He already had all of Daddy's time, was he going to take over her bedroom now, too?

She decided it was time he got out of her bedroom. "What are you doing here?" she asked loudly enough to wake him.

Todd heard the words but didn't realize they were for him. Opening his eyes, he saw his plainly irritated sister peering down at him from her bed.

"Well?" she said, impatience stamped on her features.

"I couldn't sleep in my room," he said.

"Why not?"

"Because." He couldn't finish the sentence. *Because it's haunted?* he wondered.

"Because why," she insisted.

Gathering himself and standing, he said, "Just because." He shivered from the cold and glanced at his sister's closet. "What do you have in there? An iceberg?"

"Nothing," she said. "You're just cold because you slept without any covers on *my* bedroom floor." His intrusion infuriated her to the point that a sudden image shocked her. She imagined her brother strapped to a table with her standing over him, sharp knives arranged nearby.

Todd felt a sudden need to inspect Lilith's closet. He stepped toward the door and felt something hit him hard in the back. "Ow!" he grunted, turning back to Lilith and seeing a book on the floor at his feet. She'd thrown it at him.

"Why'd you do that?" he asked.

"Stay away from my closet," she said.

"Jeez! You're crazy!" he said and left the room.

She glared at the bedroom door after he was gone. She had felt the cold coming from her closet as well but would never admit it. She knew what it was, after all, and she knew she needed to keep it a secret. The weirdest thing was how the book had flown from a shelf into his back.

Crawling out of bed, she opened the closet

door, smiling as she saw the board glowing faintly, giving off its own cold, dim light. The air in the closet made her shiver, and she could see her breath as she leaned over to grab the board. Placing it on the bedroom floor, she opened it and gasped. The card images were still as spooky as before, but now they were no longer in order by suit. She noticed the ten of diamonds was where it had been yesterday when the card had placed itself on the board—third from the corner where the gargoyle of the four of clubs watched her.

Pulling out the cards, she began placing each one on its space on the gameboard, barely able to contain her excitement. As each card was placed in its spot, the image on the card's face altered to match the gameboard's. When she finished placing the cards, she watched as the runes gathered and produced the green smoke.

Hello again, Lilith.

Todd crept down the hallway to his bedroom, thinking of Lilith. She used to be nice. He wasn't sure what had happened, but she didn't seem the same. Arriving at his room, he found the door wide open, as he'd left it the night before. His bed was unmade, the sheets in knots. His pillow was where he left it. He took this all in at a glance. Then he froze.

The window curtains were closed.

He was certain they'd been open the night before. Positive in fact. Hadn't the belief that eyes were peering in at him caused his panic? Had one of his parents come in during the night and closed them? But why would they do that? And wouldn't they come searching for him if they had?

Stepping to the window, he grasped the curtains with both hands. His heart wanted to burst from inside his ribcage. His mouth had gone dry and the taste of copper filled his mouth, spreading to his throat and lips. Fear gnawed at his insides as he suddenly yanked the curtains open. Nothing. Nothing was there. Just the window and the yard below, visible in the dawn's dim light. Looking down, he saw the stump where the dead tree had been.

Undressing for his shower, he tried his best to forget what had happened, from the disappearing pillow to the haunting eyes glowing outside his window. He'd imagined it all. He'd panicked and started having hallucinations. Sure, the sounds and the eyes had seemed real, but they weren't. They were just hallucinations, he assured himself.

He wondered if he kept telling himself that, would he eventually believe it? Part of him thought he would, but another part, the most important one—that area of the brain where logic and reason lived—didn't.

He ran the water hotter than usual and stepped into the shower, letting the warm spray relax him as he tried to dispel the chill that seeped from every pore.

Lilith watched the smoke and felt a shiver as if she'd been softly touched in a ticklish spot. She was feeling better and better about what it had told her to do. This time the instructions were really bad, but they excited her, maybe because they were so bad. She felt—chosen.

She had asked where Abyss was from, and it told her it was not of this world, that it was communicating with her from beyond her universe. *I exist in the Void,* it told her. *I live in the Beyond.*

The Beyond. She wondered what life was like there and wished she could visit.

"Can I ever come there?"

Yes, my dear.

Her breath caught. It called her *my dear*, as if she was important and beautiful.

"When?"

Once I have become a physical being on your world.

"How do you become a physical being here?" she asked.

I must be invited inside your home.

"Is that all?"

And I must enter the body of a dead animal.

She gave the smoke a look of disgust. "Eww. What kind of dead animal? A bug?"

No, something larger and faster. The smoke paused, hanging in the air as if in thought. Then it shifted. *Like a cat perhaps.*

"We have a cat, but he's alive."

Do you now? Once again, the smoke seemed to consider what to spell out next. *Lilith, do you like talking to me?*

"Yes," she said, wondering how it didn't know that since it knew everything else about her.

Well, there's a problem you don't know about yet.

"What?"

I can maintain this form for only a few days.

"What does that mean?"

I will no longer be able to talk to you by tomorrow morning.

"What?! No!" Tears sprang to her eyes.

There is only one way for us to keep talking.

"How? I'll do anything!"

I must be invited, and only in the middle of the night. I have tapped at your brother's window, trying to see if he would be a good partner for my work here, but he would not let me in.

"I can let you in!"

Yes, you can let me in tonight. You must come to your brother's room at midnight. I will be at the window. But you must also do something in the meantime.

"What?" She felt so important being asked to help Abyss.

You must take a belt or cord. The smoke hung in the air.

"Yes?"

And tie it around the cat's neck. Then you must strangle it and leave it in your closet.

"Kill Whiskers?"

Yes, unless you wish me to go away.

She thought about it. She loved their cat, but the cat couldn't talk to her. Abyss did. She definitely didn't want Abyss to leave, and they could find another cat. The animal shelter had hundreds of them. Besides, Abyss would enter Whiskers' body and bring it back to life. She would actually be talking to Abyss in the body of

Whiskers.

"Okay," she said. She grinned as their conversation continued. Killing Whiskers would be a very bad thing, but when Abyss told her how wonderful it felt to squeeze life out of a living being, she began to look forward to it.

Todd spent his day in the garage, working on a new project that he hoped would keep his room safe, but it wouldn't be finished for at least another two or three days.

He'd been working on it for about a half hour when Lilith came into the garage. "Have you seen Whiskers?"

"No." He looked at her. "Did you put my pillow under my bed?"

"Why would I do that?"

"To make me crazy and annoy me."

"Don't be stupid. I wouldn't touch your dirty pillow." She walked out of the garage before Todd could say anything else.

Five minutes later, she found the cat sunning himself in the back yard. "There you are," she said, picking him up and carrying him to her room as Whiskers purred in ignorance.

Taking Whiskers to her room, she closed the door. Then placing the cat in his carrier with the cord wound around his neck and locking the door to the carrier, she anchored her feet against the front and pulled as hard as she could on the knotted cord, dragging the cat against the locked door, pulling harder and harder and holding him there. The cat thrashed and howled, but she kept pulling. When

Whiskers finally grew still, she checked him. He was still breathing, so she pulled on the cord until she was sure he was dead. The killing took ten minutes. She thought she might feel sad, but she didn't. Abyss had been right. Strangling the life out of Whiskers with the nylon cord had been— exhilarating. She trembled, feeling shuddering feelings she never had before as her heart slammed a quick rhythm against her rib cage.

At first Lilith said nothing at dinner when her mother asked if anyone had seen Whiskers. Then Todd mentioned Lilith had searched for him, so Lilith said she hadn't found him. Lilith noticed how easy the lie came, like breathing. Was it Abyss making it so easy now?

When Lilith sneaked into Todd's room at midnight, she found his room empty. His covers were not even mussed, so he'd never even gotten into bed. She puzzled over this until she heard a tapping at the window. Her grin spread across her face as she went to the window and threw open the curtains. Two dim spots of light greeted her. Abyss had warned her not to be frightened of the disembodied eyes.

She pushed the window up with a grunt and a gust of wind nearly knocked her over. She felt the chilling gust move past her and out the bedroom door before darting down the hallway to Lilith's room. Lilith tiptoed down the hallway to avoid waking her parents or Todd, wherever he was sleeping. When she entered her room, she saw Whiskers sitting on her bed as if she'd never strangled him.

The cat looked at her, and she heard a voice inside her head.

Good evening, Lilith. Abyss had a strong, masculine voice, like Daddy's but deeper.

"You can speak to me now?" she asked, smiling.

Yes. Through telepathy. It's much easier now that I have a body.

"Wow!" she said. It was all she could think of to say.

There is much that needs to be done.

"Like what?"

By the time Abyss finished explaining what she needed to do, Lilith was anxious for the day to begin. By the end of it, she would have her daddy—and Abyss of course—all to herself. She went to bed and finally slept, her dreams a hodgepodge of strange images she didn't understand that left her trembling in her sleep.

Dianne Landers enjoyed an occasional long morning bath. Greg would rise earlier than she did and take a quick shower, moving as if he were running seriously late. She liked to lie in the tub when time permitted, soaking in hot water with bubbles and scented oils, relaxing with her phone on the floor beside the tub, earbuds firmly in place as she listened to Mozart or Chopin. Sometimes Tchaikovsky. She relished her bath time.

This morning she had nowhere to be and nothing pressing for her to do. Greg was at work, and Todd and Lilith were happily playing. As

Dianne ran a bath, complete with oils and suds, she lit a few candles, more for their scents than for light. She climbed into the hot water, inching her way down and allowing the heat to relax her. Flame shadows flickered on the walls as Mozart filled her head. She kept the volume low, enjoying the soft tunes of the troubled genius.

When she heard the hair dryer come on, she removed the buds and opened her eyes to see Lilith standing beside the tub, the hair dryer whining in her hand. Lilith turned the lights on.

"Honey, don't come too close with that, you might drop it in the water."

"I know," Lilith said. With that, she held the appliance out and dropped it, noting her mother's look of shock and surprise.

Sparks flew as Dianne's body jerked as if she had turned into a rag doll and someone was shaking her violently. The lights finally went out in the bathroom and the hair dryer became silent. Acrid smoke drifted in the room as the candles cast strange shadows on the walls.

Lilith looked at her mother's body, and one by one, she blew out the candles. She worked tears into her eyes and ran toward the garage, screaming for her brother, "Come quick! Mom's in trouble!"

Todd looked at Lilith's face and felt faint. She was pale and near panic. "What happened? Where is she?"

"In her bathroom!"

Todd ran up the stairs to his parents' bathroom and found his mother's lifeless body. He tried to lift her from the water, but the tub was slick with oils and suds. His mother's body seemed waterlogged, her deadweight too much for him. Regardless of that, he continued trying to lift and pull her from the water, fighting the odds despite the impossibility of his task.

Meanwhile, Lilith went to the downstairs phone and dialed 9-1-1. When the operator answered, she held the handset away and screamed, "Why did you do it?!"

"What?" the operator asked, confused.

"My brother! He killed our mom! He dropped the hair dryer into her bath! He killed her!" Lilith screamed, bringing tears with the ease of a chef bringing water to a boil.

Ten minutes later, the police and paramedics burst into the bathroom to find Todd still struggling to get his mother out of the slippery tub while he sobbed.

Lilith sat on a sofa in the den, a detective sat beside her, holding and stroking her hand to try to calm the girl.

"What happened?" the detective asked.

"He told me he wanted to kill Mom," she cried. "He said he was going to do it."

"Who said that?"

"My brother. And he did it. He finally did it!" she shouted at him and burst into tears, unable to continue.

When another officer brought Todd into the room, Lilith pointed at her brother and screamed, "Why did you do it?! Why?!"

"I didn't do anything!" he protested and looked at the detective. "She's lying!"

The officer holding Todd's arm looked at the detective on the sofa beside Lilith, who was sobbing into her hands. The detective nodded toward the front door, indicating they needed to take the boy in. The sister's story was all they needed. The boy could deny what he did until doomsday, and it wouldn't matter.

Once Todd had been loaded into the cruiser, Lilith spoke through her tears. "He told me he'd seen in a movie that if you dropped a running toaster or hair dryer or something into water in a bathtub, it would electrocute the person in the tub."

The detective turned the girl over to a female officer and went up to the bathroom with the dead body and hair dryer. He shook his head as he stared at the woman in the tub. "What a world," he said, and went about the business of dealing with the crime scene.

Greg rushed home. He'd been told there was an emergency, nothing more. A policeman met him as Greg pulled into the driveway and jumped from his car. "What happened?!"

Moments later, Greg sat stunned beside his daughter. For five minutes he could not speak for fear he would scream instead. He had to be strong for Lilith. Finally, he turned to her and said, "Why didn't you tell us?"

"He said he'd kill me, too, if I did." Lilith said around her sobs. She was surprised the tears were real and wondered how much she was in control and how much Abyss was.

"Why?" Greg asked. "Why would he do such a

thing?" He asked nobody in particular and looked at the detective. "This doesn't sound like Todd at all. He's such a gentle boy."

"He said the monsters told him to do it," Lilith said.

That night when they had returned from the police station, Greg and Lilith said good-night to each other. Greg went to the bedroom he had shared with his wife until that day and cried for the first time since hearing the news. He'd been too numb before. His wonderful wife was gone, killed by her own son. The son she'd given birth, nourishment— life to. Still dressed, he left the room and walked down the carpeted hallway to Lilith's room, hoping she'd been able to fall asleep.

When he got to the door, he stopped. Lilith was talking, as if in conversation. He thought for a moment she was talking to Belinda, her doll. He couldn't make out the words, but he heard Lilith giggle. He frowned. The sound of the laughter was like opening the refrigerator and finding a box of wrenches. The laughter and the tragedy did not go together. Opening her door, he saw she was talking to Whiskers. Lilith stopped mid-sentence, and both she and Whiskers looked at him. The glow from the overhead light reflected in the cat's eyes, making Greg shudder.

Trying for something resembling normalcy, Greg said, "Hi, Whiskers. Where you been?"

Then what remained of Greg's world finished toppling as the cat actually answered him. "Welcome to the party." He hadn't heard the words.

They had echoed inside his head, like a thought forcing its way in.

Lilith, who also heard Abyss' thought said, "Yay! Abyss is talking to you too, now!"

Greg forced himself to look away from the cat to his daughter. "Abyss?"

"Yeah, he's from the Beyond. I didn't think he'd talk to you, but he will." She looked at the cat with love and pride. "Isn't that great?" She turned back to her father. "He's been telling me how much fun it is to burn things. He thinks I should burn down this old house. That you could build a better one."

Greg ran to his daughter, scooped her into his arms and ran for the car. The cat followed. As they ran, Greg managed to avoid tripping over the cat that seemed to be doing its best to trip him. He grabbed and held the banister to avoid falling blindly down the stairs. He jumped into the car with Lilith, who was protesting that her father shouldn't be scared. Tossing his daughter into the passenger seat, he fumbled his keys out of his pocket, jammed them into the ignition, and revved the motor.

Greg startled when the cat jumped into the back seat of the car through an open window, hissing. As the cat pounced on Greg, digging its claws into his scalp and burying its teeth into the side of Greg's neck, Lilith screamed.

Ignoring the pain and the blood flowing from his torn flesh, Greg reached up and grabbed the cat, squeezing it as hard as he could. A cacophony of confused sounds assaulted his ears as Lilith screamed, the cat howled, and whatever was speaking through the cat yelled obscenities, demanding to be released, swearing to take Greg with him back to Hell.

Greg brought the cat to his lap and wrapped both hands around its neck. The cat's back legs dug into his arms, flailing and ripping the flesh open, soaking his arms and the cat's fur in blood. The cat tried to sink its teeth into Greg's hands, but he had a firm grip on the cat's throat, squeezing. A sudden, cold gust of wind seemed to come from nowhere, and Greg was left holding the limp body of the cat.

Staring down at the carcass, Greg tried to get control of his breathing and his thoughts. Lilith continued to scream, but he ignored her for the moment. He stared down at the cat, wondering what the Hell had just happened.

Lilith continued crying and screaming as she reached out to take the lifeless body. She cuddled him to her, wailing and sobbing and calling his name. "Whiskers! Whiskers! I'm sorry! I didn't mean to! I'm sorry!" She felt as though she had just awakened from a dream. The memory of what she'd done to her mother slammed into her, and words failed her. She sobbed into the cold fur and wanted to die.

Pulling the sobbing Lilith into his bleeding arms, Greg slowly got out of the car and carried her inside, making her leave the cat's carcass in the car for him to bury later. He would be up all night trying to figure out how to get Todd out of jail and keep his daughter from going there. Perhaps he could arrange for a mental hospital where Lilith could get help. But he wasn't even sure of that.

Wouldn't he need help too? He'd heard the voice of something inside their former pet, a voice Lilith heard as well. Were they both crazy?

Picking up the phone, he called the police, wondering how much of what had just happened he would tell them.

Several hours later on the other side of the world in Jerusalem, Farida Qureshi lay in bed, listening to the tapping at her bedroom window. The soft October night lay beyond, and Farida was frightened. She wondered if the sound might be a bird. Sometimes birds would fly into a window, but this was a tapping, as if someone or something was out there, trying to get her attention. She imagined a malevolent beast slouching in the darkness, waiting for her.

Cringing, she tried to ignore the repetitive sounds, but they wouldn't stop. Rising from her bed, Farida ventured to the window to attempt seeing what was out there. She saw nothing. Then curiosity got the better of her and she opened the window.

A sudden gust of wind surprised her. It was cold and felt like death.

THE THIRTEENTH PAINTING

Author's note: This story won first place for short fiction in the Virginia Writers Club's Golden Nib Awards. It's a bit on the dark side, sort of like the story "Abyss" that appears earlier in this book, but I am one of those people who sometimes enjoy feeling a chill run up their spine.

In her art studio where her son had once slept, Lisa stared at the canvas. She had finished a painting earlier that day and was eager to start another. Over three years she had given birth to sixty-two paintings. The early ones weren't that good—she knew that—but she recognized how she'd improved.

Her thoughts wandered to her life with Jim, her husband. They were nearly broke. He was working two jobs already and might have to work a third. She couldn't work. Well, she could, but her days were so wrapped up in Davey, their son. Their dead son, she corrected. Now, she spent her time in her studio, a place she never allowed Jim to enter, padlocking the door closed, something Jim had reluctantly agreed to.

Davey had died three years ago. A hit and run. He would be six now. Sure, being a mother had been hard. She'd been so frustrated at her apparent failures as a mother sometimes as she tried to deal with the terrible twos and his growing independence at age three. This had caused some resentment, which made her feel all the worse when he'd died. Lisa wondered if he'd be alive today if she'd been a better mother. She'd always felt guilt over his death. She'd been at home and could have kept him with her. Instead, she'd sent him to his death.

Jim had been at work, and Lisa was home because she took leave on a teacher workday. Ms. Barton, the lady who babysat Davey and four other children, had lost track of him while making their lunch. Davey had wandered outside because Ms. Barton had forgotten to re-latch the door when she'd come in with the mail. His explorations had taken him to the highway. Nobody saw what happened, and his life had ended there on the side of Highway 42. In a way, her life had ended there, too.

Davey had been named for both their fathers: David Franklin Murray. She had agreed to include Franklin, Jim's father's name, in order to be able to name their son after her father. Jim wouldn't have gone for it otherwise. However, she'd insisted her father's name come first. Jim's father was a creep. To this day, Jim had no idea what his father had tried to do at their wedding reception. She still felt nauseous when her father-in-law was around. She could often feel where his hands had groped her as if those hands were now ghosts but still active.

She'd left her teaching job. Now, all she wanted to do was paint. She'd converted his bedroom to a studio in his honor.

Her first subjects were always Davey. She had

painted thirteen pictures of him in the first eight months after—well, after. She stopped painting him when she realized the pictures were becoming too dark—not only in color but in their presentation. The last painting of him had looked like the famous Dorian Gray. In it, Davey's skin seemed to be sliding down his cheeks; his mouth stood open in a howl reminiscent of Munch's *The Scream*; his stare was both haunted and haunting. She had been unable to destroy the painting, but it was stored in the closet, the frightening image of her dead son facing the back wall.

And she did her best to ignore the whispering that drifted from behind the closet door.

A part of her knew this was impossible. Paintings didn't talk. They were just a mixture of chemicals that produced pigment arranged on a canvas to create a picture. But if pictures couldn't talk, why did this one insist on speaking to her?

Lisa had heard of artists going mad. Van Gogh had severed his own ear; Richard Dadd had spent time in the infamous Bedlam, a psychiatric hospital in England; Goya himself reported hearing voices; and Rothko and de Staël, along with Van Gogh, had taken their own lives following struggles with madness. Part of her recognized she might be losing her mind. Another part listened to the voice from the closet.

She distracted herself by visualizing what this new, empty canvas would look like when finished. Deep red and the blue-black of night formed as she imagined the finished work. She saw cliffs and a car. Ocean filled the distance, with dark greens and blues and black, whitecaps foaming as waves reached skyward. The sky was a brewing tempest, dark purple and black with bright gray and white streaks highlighting the bellies of the clouds with the buried lightening.

Lisa mixed a dollop of red with blue until the shade of purple she saw on the bare canvas filled a corner of her palette. Pulling a clean, dry brush from a jar, she stabbed the paint and began to bathe the top third of the canvas with the angry color, using swirling movements to create the sense of motion and turmoil she saw in the clouds.

Her hand moved quickly, like a conductor pulling violent music from an orchestra. Her mind entered the void where it dwelled when she was possessed with a work of art.

The background of the storm begun, she started work on the ocean. She added a few drops of white to lighten the purple she'd used for the sky and used quick, curved strokes to paint what she considered the bodies of the waves, which undulated in her mind like a woman caught in the throes of forbidden sex. Finally, she mixed new colors to paint a cliff edge in the foreground. She would add the trees, and other details later to provide perspective, along with the car in the foreground, sitting on the cliff's edge as if watching the approaching storm.

With the three major background components of the painting begun, she worked on shadings and other details of the clouds.

"Moooommyyyy."

The whispering began. While her heart beat a

fast rhythm, she did her best to ignore it.

"Moooommy. Please. I want out."

"Go away." She blushed because she had started talking to the voice several weeks ago.

"I want out. Please?"

"I can't."

"Please?" The voice—no not a voice, her son—began to weep.

She stood there, staring at the closed closet, wondering if she would be able to see the image of her dead son speak if she brought the painting out. Would the painted mouth move? Would it reshape itself from the oval of *The Scream* into words being spoken?

The crying continued, growing louder, more insistent. Davey had been like that. He would start out whimpering before the small cries quickly worked their way up to wails that had unnerved her from the start. The ceaseless crying. The torment. The baby that seemed to hate her to the point of causing torture instead of giving love.

As the cries from the painting began their slow crescendo, she realized she would have to take the painting out of the closet. It had never cried before. It had only spoken despicable things to her. Now, she had to make it stop crying.

Going to the closet door, she stood there, listening as the crying intensified.

"Stop," she begged, careful not to be too loud. If Jim walked in, he would wonder what was going on. She instinctively knew he would not hear the crying. "Please stop crying."

"Then let me out," the voice pleaded.

"If I let you out, will you stop?"

"Yes. Just let me out. Please."

Steeling herself, she grasped the knob. Then turning it, she yanked the door open as all went silent. Reaching toward the back, she grabbed the offending painting, pulling it out of its vault. She had to look at it. Had to see if the mouth had changed.

Her eyes had squeezed shut and she slowly opened them, expecting to see a painting of her son as he looked when alive, not the hideous creation she'd painted over two years ago.

But it was worse. The painting had changed, but not how she'd thought it would. Staring back at her was a demon. A grotesque image of a devil from Hell. It had three tongues, like a mockery of the Holy Trinity. The tongues were flames shooting from the devil's mouth; the eyes, orange and yellow like flames themselves, accused and condemned; the face itself was a repulsive mask of red, green, black, and yellow; ram's horns twisted from its bald crown in a threatening spiral.

Then the painted mouth moved, the tongues of fire seeming to lick the corners of the horrid lips. "Why, Mommy?"

An unwanted image from the past, forgotten or ignored until now, surfaced in her mind like a drowned body floating up from the sea's depths to bob at the surface for all to see.

She was driving along the highway on her way to pick up her son from Ms. Barton's. She had received a call that her son's pediatrician had been forced to reschedule an important appointment, moving it to that day, so she needed to pick him up early to take him to the doctor. It had been an inconvenience she could have done without. After all, Davey was at the sitters to allow her a restful day off.

As she approached the house, she saw Davey in the yard. She watched as he moved toward the road, arms stretched toward the cat skittering across the highway. No other cars were in sight as she pressed the accelerator instead of the brake.

The look on Davey's face as he recognized his mother's car would haunt her forever. He'd smiled, unaware of the danger. The thud sounded like the slamming of a coffin lid. She watched as the fragile body flew through the air in slow motion, landing beside the road in a heap of broken bones and slaughtered organs. She knew he was dead or would be soon, so she went home, trying to remember if she meant to press the accelerator or the brake.

By the time she arrived home, her cell rang. Lisa answered as if she knew nothing of what had happened. It was Ms. Barton of course, screaming frantically and punctuating her shouts with regretful apologies. Oddly, hearing someone else say her son had been hit by a car brought the first tears, as if she had planned the entire episode. But of course, she couldn't have. How could she know Ms. Barton would not latch the door and Davey would be stepping into the road as she arrived?

When Lisa approached the car to drive to the hospital, she noticed the damaged fender. As she parked at the hospital, she rammed into a car in the space in front of her, hiding the damage caused

196

when her car had struck her son.

"Why?" The words from the flaming lips brought her back to the present.

"I'm sorry," she said.

Putting the evil creation back into the closet, she went to the bathroom as if pulled by invisible strings, and undressed. Climbing into the tub, she took the box cutter she used in her artwork and split both arms open from elbow to wrist, slicing veins and an artery. She expected pain, but she felt nothing. As the blood geysered rhythmically, she gouged both femoral arteries.

After the funeral, Jim's pastor did his best to offer words of comfort. "She was just too damaged from the death of your son. Mothers often feel guilt over such things."

Jim looked at the reverend with eyes too tired from crying to shed another tear. He wondered about the enormity of the guilt necessary to do what Lisa did, especially after three years. He considered things he could have done differently. Was he the reason? Had his nagging that she find a job driven her over the edge? Was her art that important to her?

When he'd finally cut the padlock and entered his son's former bedroom for the first time since Lisa had converted it to an art studio, he'd found thirteen identical paintings of Davey along with a variety of other works that felt dark and forbidding. However, his son's sweet smile was captured perfectly in each of the portraits of him. Jim wondered why she'd painted so many, especially since they all seemed to be copies of each other. Wasn't one enough?

POETRY AND
PERSONAL ESSAYS

NOWHERE SPECIAL

Alright, maybe I lied.
I *didn't* think of you
while driving nowhere special.
I thought of how we know we have souls
because we hear songs
so beautiful
they burn our eyes—
and break our hearts—
and make us believe in
perfect.
I thought of the fields I passed,
stretching to the edge of sight,
and how a million shades of green live there.
Beauty surrounded me,
pierced into me,
and—
Alright.
Perhaps I didn't lie.

April 2018

EARLY APRIL TREES

Chilled bare trees,
like the brittle bones of old men,
reach up to the heavens
in mute supplication.

Promised leaves,
like delayed answers to prayers,
hold back until the trees plead,
"Clothe me."

Lilting birdsong,
like the music of flutes, violins, a choir,
provide warmth but no shelter
beyond their tunes.

"Please," cry the trees,
"we are old men."

April 2018

OUR JOBS DO NOT DEFINE US

This was written when I was substitute teaching before I was able to move into writing fulltime. It is self-explanatory.

After retiring from teaching, I used to substitute teach to make a few extra dollars. I shared my writing career with the people at the schools where I worked, and one day the secretary in charge of subs told me that one of their night custodians was also a writer who was working on his own graphic novel. I requested she ask the custodian to stop by the room where I would be at the end of the day. She did, and I was amazed at his work.

His name is James Muse. (I love his name!) He showed me the graphic novel he was working on. His artwork and the story and characters were as good as anything to be found in a store selling graphic novels.

This interaction made me start thinking how much we judge others by the job they hold. Yes, Mr. Muse is not college-educated, nor does he hold what most people believe to be a high-paying job, but to dismiss him because of what he does to earn his living would ignore who he is beyond his job.

This man is an artist and writer. I was enthralled by the attention to detail in his artwork.

His characters were unique and their personalities and "super powers" demonstrated genius-level imagination. I won't discuss the particulars because there are those out there who would steal his ideas and I don't wish to be a party to that, but I was captivated by the ingenuity shown in their creation.

James Muse might make his living cleaning the messes left behind by teenagers and adults alike, but I felt honored to be shown his work, which is still incomplete. I mentioned he should contact publishers of these types of work, that I thought his work was as good as anything out there, but he demurred.

We should all learn that there is more to anyone than meets the eye. Down deep we know this to be true, but we don't practice this as often as we should, and Mr. Muse was a reminder to me that I am as lax as anyone concerning reserving judgment at times.

I've seen Mr. Muse again since that day. He stopped by to say hello the last time I was at the school. I invited him to join us at Hanover Writers Club, but he works nights and will be unable to attend.

That's a shame, because he is as much of a writer as I am.

MEMORIES OF RICK

The following is an essay about my late brother, Rick, and the relationship we had. It is my tribute to him.

We are the sum of our memories. They gather in our minds like spices stored for later use, and they flavor our existence as our lives' clocks countdown to the final second. Like anyone with four siblings, many of my memories center on family. One sibling I love to remember is my older brother, Rick, who was born April 15, 1952. My parents always called him their "tax baby."

There are days that I think of Rick often. He died on May 3, 2010, so it's becoming "a while" since his death. To say we fought as children would be a shocking understatement. Rick could be a bit of a bully at times when we were children. I was three-and-a-half years younger, so I was his easy and constant target. Yet, it's funny how growing up can change things.

We became quite close as we aged into adulthood. I even rented a room from his family on more than one occasion when I was single since that was easier, cheaper, more fun than a roommate, and less lonely. That arrangement had the added perk of becoming a fixture in the lives of his daughters. To this day, the three of us feel extremely close because of their few childhood years I spent with them.

Some days I feel the loss of my brother considerably. It was on his birthday in 2010 that I spoke to him for the last time. There is no person on Earth I have had better times with - perhaps as good, but not better. Of course, like anyone, I recall particularly fond moments in our lives. The memories that follow, a tribute to him, are a few of them:

In the mid-1970s, I moved back to Florida from the New Orleans area. My Chevrolet Vega did not have the ability to pull a small U-Haul, even with my meager belongings at the time, so I enlisted Rick and his 6-cylinder midsize to help.

We rented a small trailer for a "local" move because it was cheaper than a one-way move, though it may have been illegal at the time, but the statute of limitations prevents prosecution now, so I'm safe. Leaving one night in mid-February for the drive to the west side of New Orleans, we drove overnight to our destination. I forget the exact time we left, but it was near midnight. It was also cold, in the mid-twenties.

What we didn't count on was the gas consumption when pulling the trailer. The distance from my hometown of Ft. Walton Beach, Florida, to our destination of Kenner, Louisiana, which is on the far western edge of the metro area of New Orleans, was about 260 miles. We started with a full tank and my mother's Union 76 credit card. I doubt we had forty cents between us. By the time we got to Gulfport, Mississippi, perhaps 170 miles from home, we were forced to find an open gas station. It was the middle of the night, around 3 A.M., and we were lucky to finally locate a place that was open. Keep in mind, not everyone was open 24 hours back then, and a gasoline shortage added to our problem.

Gassed up, we continued to New Orleans. After a couple of hours, we were approaching the exit off I-10 that leads into Slidell, Louisiana, just as you are getting on the six-mile-long Interstate-10 bridge that crosses the eastern side of Lake Pontchartrain. At this exit a large Union 76 station/truck stop sat with all the gas we could need. All we had was the gas card, and it wasn't good at any other places along our route. We had almost a half tank of gas in the car - as I said, the gas mileage was abysmal - but we decided to retrieve my few belongings and stop on our way back.

Big mistake.

After loading my things in the small U-Haul, we headed back toward the Union 76 near Slidell, the only Union 76 station in the New Orleans area at the time. Just as we topped the rise on the I-10 bridge, the car sputtered and quit. Rick put the car in neutral to allow it to roll until it stopped.

If you've ever been on this bridge, you know that it is actually two separate bridges, one for westbound traffic, another for eastbound. Although we had no gas can, the card could be held for ransom, so that wouldn't be a problem. But did I mention it was cold? A lighted time-and-temperature sign in Kenner had said it was twenty-two degrees - without the wind. We flipped a coin to see who would go get the gas. Rick lost the coin-flip. Bundling himself in his thin jacket, he stepped out, glared at me as if it were all my fault, which in a way I guess it was, and started walking, sticking his thumb out for a ride.

The second car to pass stopped for him, figuring out our problem since the car was parked right beside him in the breakdown lane. I sat and waited.

Of course, it was possible to hitch a ride to the gas station at the end of the bridge, get the gas, thumb a ride to the New Orleans end of the bridge, cross over, and finally thumb a ride to the car, but that would require finding two people willing to have a young man with shaggy, long hair and a smelly gas can in their car. Not likely.

So I watched and finally saw a speck in the distance: Rick, carrying the half-full, three-gallon gas can as he walked facing traffic.

I got out of the car, bundled myself against the surprisingly strong and bitterly cold wind blasting over Lake Pontchartrain, and set off to meet him, feeling the least I could do would be to carry the gas can the rest of the way once we met somewhere on that freezing bridge. The wind chill had to be near or below zero. Rick appreciated the gesture.

We filled up at the Union 76 of course, once we got the car running, and stopped again at our previous oasis when the gas level dropped to a half-tank in Gulfport.

The adventure was not fun at the time, but it was memorable, and remembering it is fun. Had I known what a special memory this would be, I would have tried to enjoy it more back then. But back then, we thought we'd live forever.

Another memory of Rick also involved New Orleans. He was on his way from one place to another by air, and he purposely set up a long layover so we could have some time together. I was living in Metairie at the time, a suburb of New Orleans, and after I picked him up from the airport, we drove downtown to have some beignets and coffee from the original Cafe du Monde in the French Quarter. Our plan from there was to wander around the Quarter and see what we could see.

We ended up strolling around Jackson Square, which is right across the street from Cafe du Monde, and Rick decided to sit for a portrait. The artist *assured* us he would be done in plenty of time for Rick to get to the airport and catch his flight. When the man was *finally* finished, it was obvious Rick would probably miss his flight, but we decided to try anyway.

We ran to where we parked the car as I wondered if someone might think we'd just committed a crime, I paid the attendant for parking, and Rick took my keys and pulled my car up to the lot exit to pick me up. We ran several stop lights on Canal Street, somehow avoiding getting a ticket. These lights were not "maybe red" lights; they were red - with cars waiting. Rick would pull around the cars and speed past them when it was clear enough to shoot between oncoming cars to our right and left, only to be forced to do the same at the next light. When we merged onto I-10, Rick zoomed in and out of traffic.

We finally arrived at the airport, which is about fifteen miles from the French Quarter. Rick told me to circle around and if he'd missed his flight, which was scheduled to leave about twenty minutes before we had arrived, he would be outside waiting for me. If he wasn't there, I could go home.

I circled around to find Rick standing on the sidewalk, waiting for me. Instead of jumping in, though, he told me his flight was delayed an hour, and he had plenty of time. (Keep in mind that getting to the gate was not the hassle it is today.) Lucky break! We both could breathe again.

The next day, I went out to get in my car to go to work and found a flat tire waiting for me. All I could think was how lucky we were it hadn't happened the day before. I only wish I knew what became of that picture of Rick. It was a good one, done in chalk, and I'd love to have it, or at least be able to give it to his daughters.

Finally, anyone who knows me well is aware I am a dyed-in-black-and-gold New Orleans Saints fan and have been since the day they began playing in the NFL in 1967. Rick, on the other hand, ended up in Tampa for his final years and became a Buccaneers fan. I forgave him. But in the last years of his life, he became quite ill and had to use an electric scooter style of wheelchair to get around. I would visit him every summer, and we would do as much as we could together. One year we went to Busch Gardens to enjoy the rides, but the best time was the year we attended The Tampa Bay Bucs training camp in Orlando.

We loaded his truck with the scooter and set off. Arriving at the sports complex where Jon Gruden led the Bucs in their training camp, we pulled up in time to see the last forty-five minutes of practice. When we got there, Rick bought an official NFL Tampa Bay Bucs football. I bought a t-shirt for my son-in-law, who is also a Bucs fan. (Don't worry; I've forgiven him too.)

When practice was over, several players stuck around to sign autographs. We managed to have everyone there sign the football and shirt, though there weren't that many players staying out to sign.

The most gracious among the players was Ike Hilliard, who happens to be the nephew of a former New Orleans Saint, Dalton Hilliard, a star running back for the Saints in the late 1980s and early 1990s. He went from fan to fan, talking with them, posing for pictures, etc. He was, at that time, nearing the end of a good career as a wide receiver, and his willingness to spend time with his fans in the Florida heat amazed me. He remained long after all the other players had gone inside to shower and enjoy the air conditioning after a long, hard practice.

As he moved from one place to another to sign autographs and chat, Mr. Hilliard would say to Rick, "Don't go anywhere. I'll get with you before you leave." He did this at least three times.

When he finally made his way to us, he explained he wanted Rick to be his last fan so he could spend as much time with him as Rick wanted. Rick, remember, was in an electric scooter/wheelchair because of his illness, which was apparent to anyone who looked at him. (He was truly skin-and-bones.) Mr. Hilliard talked with Rick, allowed me to take as many pictures of them as I wanted, telling me not to worry as I fumbled nervously with the camera, and signed both the football and the t-shirt. I "confessed" to being a Saints fan, and told Mr. Hilliard to thank his uncle for me for all the great runs when he saw him again. He was a pleasant and wonderful man to someone who obviously was not going to be on this earth for many more years. Rick, of course, loved every second of it, and we thanked Ike Hilliard for keeping us for last so the man wouldn't feel rushed to get to anyone else. A class act.

So, those are three of the fondest memories I have of Rick. He had a great life, but he died far too young. That's what happens when you live in such a way as to flame out. He enjoyed "having fun" a bit too much for his own good. But he enjoyed every second of his life that he could, too.

NOVEL EXCERPT

FIRST CHAPTER OF *SAVING TWIGS*

Here is the first chapter of my novel, Saving Twigs. I borrowed the first paragraph of this book from my short story "Accidental Rendezvous," so that will sound familiar to those who read that story, which appears on page 83 of this book. Yes, if I wrote it, I can do that. I hope the first chapter of this novel touches something inside you.

I love walks, especially on warm, breezy days like today when the sun is so bright it's blinding even when you don't look right at it. Mama says the sun gave me my red hair. She says one day the sun just reached right down and touched it and it turned into the flaming red it is now. I used to believe her, but I'm too old for that now.

Anyway, I'm on a walk right now to think about things, especially the last two years. I imagine I will be taking a lot of these walks to figure it all out and get perspective, as my grandma would say. I needed perspective because it might be the only thing that will keep me sane after all that has happened. What I'm telling you will start out light, like any thirteen-year-old girl's life, but I have to warn you—it gets pretty heavy later on, ending with a funeral.

I guess I should tell you a little about myself before I get into all the stuff that brought me to this point. I'm fifteen now, but what I'm going to tell you about started back when I was thirteen. Funny how it seems like yesterday but it doesn't. Time plays a lot of tricks on us. At least, that's what Grandma says. Two years ago seems like forever, but it also seems like last week. Like I said, it's funny how time is like that. Grandma says it gets worse as I grow older. Great. Another thing to not look forward to.

My name is Maureen Lindstrom. I'll go ahead and tell you I hate that name. It's not that I hate the name Maureen. It's just that I never met anyone else my age with that name because it sounds old-fashioned, but my Mom insisted on naming me after her grandmother. Besides, I had that red mop of hair that reminded my mom of this actress from years ago named Maureen O'Hara. I'd go by my middle name with people my age, but that one is even worse: Dickson. Sorry, no thanks. It's not even a name, or at least not a first name, and even if it was, I wouldn't use it. I don't think I have to say why. Anyway, my mom insisted on giving me my dad's middle name. So back on July 27, 2004, I was born in Pensacola, Florida, where my mom lived at the time, and given two names I would hate forever. Yeah, lucky me.

I never actually met my dad. He was a cop who was killed when he went to a domestic disturbance call before I was born. He knocked on the door and the guy inside opened the door holding a gun and shot my dad before he had a chance to say anything. At least that's what my mom said happened. My dad's partner shot the guy who killed my dad. I'm not sure how I feel about that, really. I mean, I know he was my dad and all, but I also never met him. It's weird.

My mom married my dad when they were both twenty-one, and I was born a year later. Her name is Brandy Marie (another reason for "Maureen") Shaw Lindstrom. She owns a local flower shop. She says she got interested in plants working for a lady when she was a teenager after she got in some trouble and managed to be found innocent of the crime.

Since I know you're going to be curious about that, I'll tell you that she ran over a guy who had more or less taken her prisoner. She ran off with the guy when she was all confused about things in her life at the time. I asked her if she did it on purpose, and she says she doesn't know because she doesn't actually remember doing it. I asked if she was drunk or high on something, but she says she wasn't. Just scared. He was robbing this place in Jacksonville, Florida, and she was supposed to drive getaway. She'd only driven a car a couple of times before, and she was in a terrible life with this creep. He actually would lock her in the small apartment they shared and be gone all day. He would steal cars and sell them for a living. Yeah, I know. A real prince.

I asked her the guy's name, but she wouldn't tell me. She said he didn't deserve a name. I can't say as I blame her.

Now, we live in Denton, Florida, where my grandma moved to when my mom was my age now. Grandma moved them all to Florida so she could marry a man she ended up divorcing a few years later.

My Uncle Ryan is in the Air Force, stationed at Ramstein Air Base in Germany. I think he's lucky, but he says he'd rather be, as he puts it, "stateside." He's nice to me whenever we can see him. He's married and has twin sons a year older than me and a daughter who's twelve. I like Uncle Ryan's wife, but I barely know my cousins since I've only seen them about six or seven times in my life.

Anyway, I guess that's enough about me. You'll learn more about me as I tell you my story.

Like I said, though, what I'm going to tell you about happened two years ago. I was only thirteen and sort of lonely for friends. I mean, I had friends, but I was getting sort of tired of the ones I had. None of them were like besties or anything, and I guess I wanted someone like that.

The weird part was the bestie I ended up meeting was a guy. I know that may not sound all that weird, but it felt like it, especially at the time. A thirteen-year-old girl has a lot of stuff she needs to talk about, some of it kind of private, so I was needing another girl to talk to about life and relationships. As it turned out, maybe he needed a bestie more than I did.

Anyway, it all started when I had just turned thirteen. My body was changing and life seems to sort of rush itself along when that starts happening like there's this race to see how fast childhood can crumble into dust. I know I was wanting things to slow down a bit, but of course, that wasn't happening. As my mom said, you can't stop nature from moving at its own pace.

I remember it was right after my grandmother moved in with us. I know a lot of girls get along with their grandmothers like bees and honey, but that's not the way it is with me. Grandma and I butted heads like crazy. It seemed like everything I wanted to do she didn't like.

Wear makeup? You're too young.

Wear ragged blue jeans? You're too pretty.

Go on dates? You're too gullible.

I had to look that one up on my phone, and its meaning made me mad. Did she think I was stupid or something?

Anyway, it was like that all the time, and the worst part was my mom took her side. Every. Single. Time.

I called a girl named Cameron that I knew from my science class to complain, but she was like, we all have to deal with that. Well, that wasn't what I wanted to hear, so I decided I needed a real bestie who would get mad about it like me.

One thing I had to be careful with was picking the wrong person to tell my secrets to. I liked Cameron, but she could be a blabbermouth. She wasn't cruel about it. She just sometimes told things she shouldn't tell, like the time she told about another girl telling her about a secret crush. I needed a bestie I could trust to keep quiet about things.

Then, as if my wish was being granted by some fairy godmother or something, the very next day in school, I met Nick.

Nick's family had just moved to Denton, and that was his first day at our school. He was put at

217

the table in science class that I shared with two other girls, the girl I had called the night before named Cameron and Mia, who was so boy crazy she made me want to apologize for the rest of the feminine world.

Don't get me wrong. I like boys and did back then, too, but I've never been out of my mind over some guy. That's probably because of what happened to my mom when she was a teenager and described herself as a lot like Mia. My mom raised me to believe no guy is worth losing my mind over, no matter how much being around him made me feel, as she put it, "all melty."

"There are plenty of nice guys out there, like your dad. You just have to do a lot of searching to find one good enough to devote yourself to," she'd told me about a thousand times. Anyway, I guess her words stuck.

Mia, on the other hand, was like my mom when she was a teenager. Some guy would walk by her, and she'd roll her eyes with what can only be described as a "wanting." I thought it was the personification of insanity.

Cameron was sort of like me, except she wasn't real bestie material for me, like I said.

So, needless to say, when Nick was introduced to the class as a new student from Michigan, Mia looked like she was about to start drooling. Cameron looked at me and just shrugged at Mia's obvious flirting the second Nick sat down, as if to say, *we all have to deal with that*.

I suppose Nick was good-looking with his shock of dark brown hair that flipped across his forehead and shy smile, but I was not really attracted to him. I wasn't even thinking of him becoming a bestie candidate. He just seemed like a nice guy.

One thing was he barely said three words that first class. A lot of guys would try to talk up Mia at least, given her obvious attraction reaction. Nick just sort of stayed to himself.

At lunch that day, Mia was going on about how lucky it was that Mr. Clay seated Nick at our table.

"Mia, we had the only empty seat in the class," I reminded her, but her response remained focus on the luck.

"I know! Wasn't that lucky?!"

I spied Nick sitting at a lunch table by himself the next day and invited him to join us. I would have sat alone with him, but first that would start rumors flying like rolls in a food fight, and second, Mia would have hated me forever because she would think I was after Nick for myself.

"Hey," I said after approaching the otherwise empty table where he sat. "Want to come sit with us?"

He looked up at me, looking puzzled like I was asking him the answer to a particularly difficult math problem. Then I guess he recognized me and said, "Sure." No smile. No look of gratitude. Nothing. Just "sure."

He followed me to where Mia was drooling and Cameron was whispering to Mia, probably trying to get her to tone it down a bit.

As he sat, Mia said, "Hey! What part of Michigan are you from?" as if she knew the state's geography.

"Grand Rapids."

"Cool!" Mia gushed. "Is that near Detroit?"

"Not really. It's on the other side of the state, not that far from Lake Michigan."

Any fool could tell he wasn't interested in Mia the way she was interested in him. Okay, nobody could be interested in anyone quite the way Mia was interested in Nick, but what I'm saying is he didn't seem interested in any kind of teenage romance, especially with Mia. She, of course, hadn't noticed his lack of interest in her at all.

"So, tell us about Grand Rapids!" Mia continued. "Tell us about your friends there. What are they like?"

Mia was obviously fishing for info on a possible love interest he left behind, but he wasn't cooperating.

He shrugged. "Not much to tell."

"Well, you had friends, didn't you?" Cameron asked, obviously ready to feel bad for him if he was friendless in Michigan.

"Yeah. I just don't like to talk about people when they're not around."

Okay, this was different. Most kids our age would rather talk about other people than go to a movie, which was a big reason we liked to gather together at places like movie theaters in the first place.

I think this was my first inkling that he might be bestie material. He apparently had no interest in blabbing secrets, even to people who didn't know the people whose secrets he would be blabbing.

I said, "You'd make a great spy."

That was the first time he really smiled at me. It wasn't a flirty smile, just a nice one. He seemed to appreciate the compliment.

When I looked over at Mia, she was looking daggers at me.

The conversation went on like that until we had to go to our next class. Mostly Mia asking questions and Nick doing his best to say as little as possible.

My next class was English with Ms. Henderson, so we all parted to go our separate ways, or at least I thought we did. Nick asked where Ms. Henderson's room was. I glanced at Mia before answering. I knew she wouldn't like this, but what was I going to do? Be rude and not tell him I was headed there myself?

"I'm going there myself," I said.

"Great," he answered, and we walked past a fuming Mia toward our next class.

As it happened, my fairy godmother was at work again without my knowing it since the seat in the row next to where I sat was empty, and Ms. Henderson allowed us to choose where we sat. Our choice, though, wasn't a "change your seat every day" thing. Once we made a choice, that was our seat unless she moved us or we asked permission to move.

As we entered the room, I said, "The seat next to mine is open if you want to sit there."

"Won't the teacher tell me where to sit?" he asked.

I explained Ms. Henderson's "choose your own seat" policy.

He shrugged, as if he couldn't care less where he sat and took the empty seat in the row next to where I sat.

He began readying himself for class, so I did the same. After the bell rang and Ms. Henderson asked Nick to introduce himself, which he did as quickly as possible—"Hi, I'm Nick"—I began to wonder why I wasn't falling for him the way Mia was. I could tell from the glances of some of the other girls in class that he was definitely considered a prize, but I had no interest in that at all. In fact, if he'd asked me out on a date, I would have gladly informed him that my mother wouldn't allow me to date yet as an excuse to let him down gently. I'm not a guy, but I can imagine how devastating it is to ask a girl out only to be told by the girl she isn't interested in him "in that way." It's like telling him, "Sorry, but I think you're ugly and uninteresting."

After English, he asked me where his next class was, and I was actually kind of glad it wasn't the same one I was going to. That would have felt *really* weird, as if my fairy godmother was trying to tell me I needed to fall head-over-heels in love with him or something.

When I finally arrived home that afternoon and started on my homework after a snack, I found myself thinking of Nick. Not in a boyfriend kind of way but a friend kind of way. I was starting to realize he might be a really good friend to have.

It wasn't until months later I found out he had been thinking of me in the same way at the same time because as it turned out, he was really in need of a bestie as well. But for him it was about more than just having someone to talk to. It was urgent for him, even if neither of us realized how urgent at the time.

ABOUT THE AUTHOR

Charles Tabb lives with his wife, two dogs, and his wife's two horses near Richmond, Virginia. Besides writing and reading, he loves traveling and spending time with family.

You can purchase other books by the author, listed earlier in this book, by going to his website at https://charlestabb.com. While there, you may also want to sign up for his brief, monthly newsletter, Haunted by the Muses. In this newsletter, he talks about what he is working on as well as makes suggestions for reading in various genres. The newsletter is conversational in tone and a pleasant, short read.

Charles Tabb is available for speaking engagements. You may contact him through the CONTACT link on his homepage. Zoom appearances and most in-person talks are free.

Made in the USA
Middletown, DE
09 December 2022